NULL_POINTER

A Joshua Jones Mystery

by

Ken McConnell

This is a work of fiction. All of the characters, organizations, and events depicted in this novel are products of the author's imagination.

GB Press
http://gbpress.ning.com

NULL_POINTER

ISBN is 978-0-578-02613-8

First Edition: August 2009

Printed in the United States of America
Cover art and layout by Byron McConnell

The Official Null_Pointer web site: http://nullpointer.ning.com
The author's blog: http://w0pht.org/wordpress

For my dad, Gerry McConnell

TECHNICAL ADDENDUM

The Amateur Radio call signs used in this book are not real. They have too many letters. They were created by the author and any resemblance to actual call signs is purely coincidence and not intentional. The author does have his Amateur Radio license and can be found on local Boise repeaters from time to time.

Every effort was made to ensure the accuracy of technical details discussed in the book. Some parts of the plot involve things that cannot actually happen at the time of the writing. Successful fiction often requires a leap of faith from the reader. The author hopes that the leap is a small one for this story.

CHAPTER 0

THE PROGRAMMER CLICKED the link and slipped on his cushioned headphones. The entire screen of his monitor went blank and a low throbbing came from his headphones. The throbbing became a steady, thump-thump, thump-thump of a heart at rest. The screen came alive with a kaleidoscope of colorful shapes.

The images moved to the cardio-rhythms and as the beat quickened so did the speed of the colors and shapes. The programmer became slightly agitated. The soothing images faded into rougher shapes with harder edges and the colors became more intense. Blues and greens and browns blurred into reds and yellows. The shapes became sharp as knife blades as the rhythm sped up.

The programmer could feel his heart race to the increasing beats of the bass drum. He wanted to pull off the headphones and stop the animation but his arms were languid. Try as he might, he could not make the slightest move to stop the presentation. It was mesmerizing and he was locked in its grip.

The images faded into a fog of dark blue and gray swirling clouds. The sound echoed and reverberated, like ambient music. The programmer swore he heard a woman wailing and the wind blowing. There were other sounds, sounds of a city, cars honking, semi-trucks braking and sirens screaming in the night. The swirling clouds faded away to a black screen and the programmer fell into subconsciousness. He was floating in a world that was not his reality. It had the appearance of the real world, but it existed only in his mind's eye.

He held onto a cold, metal structure that consisted of three tubes and had cross braces every few feet. It was cold, terribly cold as the wind whipped passed him and bit into him, chilling him to the bone. The programmer had never been that cold in all his life. He shook and trembled in the blowing wind. He peered down and saw that he was perched atop a radio tower on the very top of a skyscraper.

His fear of falling returned, first experienced when he was a teenager and he jumped from a high dive into the neighborhood pool. It haunted him for months thereafter - the feeling of falling into an endless dark hole. He no longer had such nightmares, but he could never allow himself to be on a tall structure without becoming agitated to the point of distraction.

His mind ran as fast as the wind and his beating heart. How the hell did he get this far up on a tower? Was this some kind of dream? More like nightmare. It was every bit as real as anything he had ever known. There was no denying that he was thousands of feet up in the sky and afraid for his life. There was no way he was going to climb down the tower to the base of the antenna. It was too far and the wind was too strong. He was doomed to fall; it was only a matter of when.

The building swayed from the turbulent winds making him nauseous. His hands slipped; he locked his elbows around the braces of the tower and held on. A flashing navigation light above him caused his hands to glow an eerie red color. How in the hell did he get in this position? It had to be a dream. If he thought about it hard enough, maybe he would wake up. No such luck.

The programmer screamed into the wind, his voice carried away like an echo in a canyon. No one would know where he was and rescue would be impossible. His grip was loosened again. He looked down and his heart sank like a rock. He was doomed to fall. His life would be over and there was nothing he could do to help himself. Fear paralyzed him.

When the hopelessness of the situation sunk in, he was ready to fall, ready to sink into the swirling abyss, ready to let go, ready to die.

The programmer closed his eyes. The cold wind died away as his fingers slipped. The falling sensation returned. Comfort. Freedom. No fear.

CHAPTER 1

HIS MOM'S PIERCING scream echoed in his ears as her arms stiffened against the padded dashboard. His dad's eyes popped open wide as he turned back to desperately grab the wheel and regain control. Tree limbs brushed against the front window of the family car as it slid off the icy road. The car jolted hard as it tipped over and nosed into the river. Cold water shocked his system. Flailing arms thumped helplessly against the windows. Gurgling sounds. Then darkness.

Joshua Jones couldn't sleep most nights. This one was particularly bad. Every time he tried to shut his eyes the images came back as if he were stuck in some kind of real life code loop. Listening to music, turning his damp pillow over, changing his position and even the couch could not ward off the suffocating feeling of guilt he felt for his parents death.

They were driving up to their cabin in McCall, Idaho and the roads were slick with ice and snow. Joshua was sixteen and just learning to find his way around a program compiler. His dad was answering a question that Joshua had asked about programming. John Jones loved to talk with his hands and in responding to his son's question he let go of the wheel just as the car began to slip on the ice. It was only for a brief second. One careless move brought on by Joshua's question.

For the past six years Joshua blamed himself for the accident. No amount of counseling or therapy could remove the guilt he felt for their deaths. Several times a year he suffered bouts of insomnia that lasted anywhere from a few days to a week. It was no way to live, but it was the only way he knew.

The lack of sleep and complete exhaustion usually caught up with him and he was able to resume his life afterward with some degree of normality. But for those nights when the dreams held him in their painful grip, he was helpless to stop them.

Around three in the morning he gave up on sleep and tried to watch TV. Staring at sitcoms that had run the night before did not help. He left the TV on and went into his den to try coding. Sometimes it was his only refuge from the feelings of guilt. He could lose himself in the deep meditation of programming and forget the disturbing images. Over time he would begin to release his guilt, but he was never fully free from it. If he had not asked his father that stupid question, his parents would still be alive and he would not be having these horrible nightmares. That simple fact was so desperately hard for him to let go of.

There was always someone on-line at all hours of the night. The coding chat rooms he frequented were alive with chatter about obscure code constructs and light hearted banter about favorite editors. He slowly pulled himself out of his depression and started focusing on the code. There was a particularly tricky algorithm he was wrestling with at work and the solution to it popped into his head unannounced like all bursts of inspiration and suddenly he felt the need to finish it.

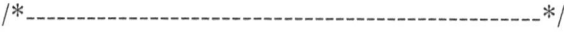

A light snow was falling as Joshua flashed his ID card at the reader and entered building four of RegTech. It was a dark morning in November and he was sure that he was the only person crazy enough to be in this early on a Friday. The white ear buds of his iPod were pumping the staccato beats of his favorite rock band into his head as he strolled past the empty cubes carrying his laptop in a shoulder pack.

He had the kind of likable face that women called cute and immature men liked to beat up. He wore a brown jacket with a hooded dark blue sweatshirt underneath. The dress standard was pretty lax at the tech company and he wore the same faded blue jeans and black Cons that got him through his college years.

Joshua's mind was not on the music. He was thinking about how to handle a tricky array construct and the music helped him to concentrate, and keep out the bad dreams. His father used to say he was part of Generation Multi-task, and always gave him a hard time about it. Joshua just shrugged it off, a body does what a body needs and his body needed music to concentrate.

As he strolled down the hall and turned down the rows of cubicles, the lights winked on a few rows ahead of him. Even a big multi-national company like RegTech had some energy conservation policies in effect. The lights may have been out from lack of movement, but the building was still a warm and cozy seventy-five degrees. Joshua started unzipping his coat before he made it to his row. He had three PC's in his cube and two big screen monitors that radiated plenty of heat. A rotary fan in the back of his cube ran constantly, to keep him cool in both summer and winter.

As Joshua strolled, he noticed the distinct aroma of Flying Pie pizza. Someone had been burning the midnight oil. Glenn, the coder in the cube next to his, sat at his computer, motionless. The pizza box lay open on his desk with a few crusts scattered about. It looked to Joshua, as he silently slipped past, like he had consumed an entire large pizza.

Joshua back stepped, peering around the padded cube wall. Yes, it really was Glenn, slouching back in his chair, head turned away, fast asleep. Joshua grinned. He continued on to his cube, slipped off his shoulder bag and slid into his chair.

With a few quick keystrokes he was logged into his computer and started working on a piece of troublesome code. It took two

days of pondering, but it worked. He made a fist and pumped it
with enthusiasm. Then he got up and grabbed his coffee mug.
It was time to make the first pot of coffee for the day. Thoughts
of his parents demise and his nightmares faded from his head.
Sometimes having an obsessively detailed job was a good thing.
It freed his mind from the mundane regularities of life.

He strode past Glenn's sleeping form and made his way
down the hall, lights winking on as he walked. As he took out
the coffee and dumped it into the filter he started to wonder why
Glenn had pulled an all-nighter on a Thursday. There were no
pressing deadlines and Glenn was not the type to come in off-
hours and work for no reason, unlike other programmers Joshua
knew at the company.

Glenn was strictly an eight to five kind of guy. And for most
of the other employees in Joshua's web group, that was fine with
them. Glenn was not the most well liked individual. He was
arrogant and loud and he always seemed to take the opposing
viewpoint in any debate. Joshua figured he just liked to argue,
but most people were put off by it. Glenn was always the first
to point out the flaws in other people, but regarded himself as
nearly perfect in everything he did.

The irony was not lost on Joshua that Glenn had been caught
snoozing at his desk, even if it were not technically during
working hours. People would be streaming in soon enough and
someone would probably find him asleep and make a big scene
about it. Joshua decided that it would not be in his best interest
to bust him this time. Glenn's cube was beside his own and
that would mean undue noise and attention throughout the day.
Better to wake him now and save himself and Glenn the grief.

Joshua left his mug at the coffee station as the fresh java
brewed and headed back. Stepping inside the entrance to Glenn's
cube, he pulled out his headphones and touched the coder on the
shoulders. The hairs on the back of Joshua's neck jumped up.
Glenn was dead.

A fact that was hard to deny when you considered how rotund the man was and how heavy people usually made a wheezing sound when they were sleeping. Glenn's body was as still as a boulder, but his chubby fingers were still wrapped around his laser mouse and his ergonomic keyboard. It was as if he had died suddenly and without any kind of a struggle.

Joshua took a deep breath as he stepped back. The memory of his parents' lifeless bodies on a slab in the morgue rushed back. Their loving faces, swollen and blue. Joshua forced the unpleasant memory from his mind and studied Glenn's cube.

Open soda cans and candy wrappers littered the messy desk. Glenn was one of those brilliant minds that couldn't be bothered with the mundane details in life, like decorating his personal space. There were no family pictures or plants on his desk other than a few old O'Reilly programming books on his shelf, technical specification papers and an industry magazine that was about two years old

Glenn's monitor was in standby mode, which meant he might have passed on some time ago. Joshua hurried back to his cube and dialed the security hot line for the building. An alert sounding man answered the phone and immediately contacted Emergency Services. A security person was dispatched and a cryptic message was soon blaring from the building's speaker system.

"Damn."

As he stared at the dead man's cube, he realized that his day was shot to hell.

Ten hours later, Joshua pulled his silver Porsche convertible into the parking garage of the apartment where he lived in downtown Boise. He was exhausted but glad to be home. Once inside he grabbed a beer and fell into his easy chair in front of his high definition TV.

Unix his cat was sitting contentedly on the back of the couch. His body was snug in the collapsed back cushion. He watched Joshua eat for a while before his eyes slowly closed. Joshua had picked up some Korean food on the way home and placed the bulgogi and kimche on his lap. He stared silently at the news and kicked off his shoes.

The consensus at work was that Glenn had suffered a massive and sudden heart attack. It was something anyone could have guessed, yet somehow it required two hours of his time at the police station and endless interruptions at work by people from all over the company who just had to stop by to get the details.

At one point Joshua was sure the police thought he was a suspect, just because he had come in early and no one else was in the building for most of the night. Nobody actually came out and suggested it, but it was just the impression he got. The cold stares from his co-workers unsettled him. Few liked Glenn that much, but he was not so bad a person as to be worth killing. He was always eating junk food and consuming Mountain Dew and energy drinks like an alcoholic who drank cheap beer. His lifestyle finally caught up with him. Joshua was no pillar of health himself, but he was a good deal younger than Glenn.

He shoved another beef strip in his mouth then followed it with a chaser of Grolsch. The Kimche was particularly hot and he guzzled down his second beer to squelch the spices. With a smile he realized he was buzzed. He stared at the life-like images on the huge TV hanging on his wall. Sometimes when he was relaxed and still he felt like it was a portal to another part of the world, like a bad sci-fi film. The picture clarity was phenomenal. He changed the channel to a nature program, transporting himself to Africa, sitting quietly in the tall grasses of the Serengeti with a den of lions.

But it didn't last long. Joshua saw the back of Glenn's head, the slightly balding scalp with thinning brown hair. Death unnerved him. Just yesterday Glenn bored him with his description about a World of Warcraft on-line gaming campaign he was leading. Try as he might, he could not remember anything that Glenn had said to him about the game, he only remembered Glenn's excitement. He could picture Glenn's face, pink skin wet with small beads of sweat and so completely full of life. But Glenn was dead. Incredibly unfair.

As tired as he was from being up the night before, the last thing he wanted to do was fall asleep and have Glenn's demise spark the nightmare of his parents' death. The TV had changed to an aquarium, showing an underwater documentary about tropical fish. He sat up and felt his beer buzz. He put the remains of his dinner aside and slowly stood. His cell phone went off in his pocket. He glanced at the phone's clock; it was just after two in the morning.

"Hello?"

"Joshua, let me in," his friend Dancia pleaded.

"Sure."

He closed the phone and opened the door. She brushed past and handed him an empty coffee container.

"Have you heard the news? A hacker was killed today."

Joshua padded along after her into the computer room.

"I know, but I wouldn't say he was a hacker, more like a hack."

She was already logged on to his main workstation and was opening an Internet Relay Chat session by the time he got to the den. She looked back at him through her black rim glasses.

"What?"

"It was Glenn from my work group. He must have had too many pizzas and Dews."

She looked at him with a curled brow.

"Glenn died?"

"Yeah, I found him dead in his cube this morning. Didn't you hear?"

She stared at him for a moment her eyes wide and then

looked back to the dual plasma screens and opened a connection to her favorite server and coding channel.

"Holy shit, I didn't know that. I've been off line until this evening. I was chatting with DrunkMonk in pound coders and he said that Zemo was found dead last night in Stuttgart."

Joshua sat down on a beanbag near the workstation.

"Wait, *our* Zemo?"

Dancia nodded as she typed. "Our interface guru for MyMovies; he was found in his room by his parents. No official cause of death. He was only sixteen. I had no idea he was that young."

It was strange that two coders that he knew had died on the same day. *What were the odds of that happening?* It never occurred to him that they had both died without apparent malfeasance.

"I wonder who will die next," Dancia said. Her voice was solemn. She had dark black hair cut in a bob and deep brown eyes behind her glasses. Her skin tone was pale white; no self-respecting geek had tanned skin, even in Idaho. She was wearing a black T-shirt that read, "There's no place like 127.0.0.1" under her black leather jacket. She wore no watch; nobody under the age of thirty did anymore. It had been replaced with the ubiquitous cell phone, hers was tucked into the front pocket of her tight low riding jeans.

Joshua shook his head and looked away. He didn't believe in superstitions, like people you know dying in threes, but *she* did so he kept his skepticism to himself.

Her voice lowered a bit, morbid curiosity creeping in.

"What was Glenn's body like?"

Joshua looked up. "Still," he said, "very still."

"You were his friend weren't you? Didn't you guys hang out together at work?"

"Yeah, I guess so. Listen, I've got to get some sleep. It's been a long day for me. You staying?" he said standing up.

She looked back to the screens. "Do you mind if I work from here tonight? I don't feel like being in my apartment alone."

He rested a comforting hand on her shoulder. "Nope, see you later."

She smiled up at him as he left and then returned her attention to the IRC chat. Dancia was always coming over and hacking on his machines at all hours of the night. She worked a night shift at the local microprocessor plant and the only time she could see her friends was when she had the day off which was usually during their night time hours.

Joshua didn't mind, he let his friends use his place. It was not unusual on the weekends to find six people crashed on the floor from an all night LAN party. He preferred that they spend the night rather than risk driving home drunk or tired or both.

Joshua padded back to his bedroom and flopped down on his bed. But he did not sleep. He lay there trying not to think about his parents. Then he took out an old composition book he used for recording his dreams. Ever since the nightmares had started after his parents death, he had found it cathartic to write down his dreams.

He read through the familiar passages. Something was not right. He flipped back further going back in time three, four and five years. Skimming through the passages, he stopped when he found it. In his dreams he used to be playing Nintendo's Game Boy before the accident, not talking about coding with his dad. Either his dreams had changed or his memory was becoming more challenged the older he got. He thought about the changes and tried to recall playing the game. Try as he might, he could not recall ever playing his Game Boy on that trip. He remembered the games he used to play, but that was all.

Finally, his weary body demanded that he sleep.

CHAPTER 2

JOSHUA WOKE TO the sounds of cartoons. He opened his eyes trying to focus on the ceiling. The afghan from his couch was covering him in a warm and cozy pocket. The LED clock beside his bed read eight thirty-five. Somehow he managed to get some sleep. Dancia usually left for work around six, so he must have dozed off long before that. He still felt tired but his mind was grudgingly awake.

Nix was lying up against him snoring. The old gray and black cat had belonged to his father. Born in the same decade as the UNIX operating system, his father named the cat Unix, but for as long as Joshua could recall, he was just called Nix. Joshua sat up and listened. From the orchestrated music and lack of voices he became convinced that it was classic Tom and Jerry.

He pulled the afghan over his shoulders and strode out into the main living area. Nix stayed on the warm spot of the bed, his head turned in towards his body. The cat rarely moved around much anymore, old age and blindness in one eye saw to that.

In the living room, Tripp was stuffing himself with a bowl of Captain Crunch cereal and laughing at the cat and mouse humor on the TV. It was just like back in college except the digs were more up-scale and the hairstyle was different. Tripp was a lean, brown haired man with a bottomless stomach and the annoying habit of eating with his mouth open.

He noticed Joshua moving into the kitchen and spoke with

his mouth full, "Sup!"

Joshua waved, found a clean coffee mug and poured himself a cup of coffee. At least Tripp had sense enough to make a full pot. After fixing his coffee how he liked it, Joshua padded into the living room and plopped down in his easy chair. The Korean take out was still sitting there, though it had been finished off and moved to the coffee table. There were a few more empty beer bottles nearby. Dancia must have helped herself.

"I love Tom and Jerry," Tripp offered, as he watched the animation.

"I know. I *still* like Looney Tunes better," Joshua reminded him.

"Do you think its crazy watching cartoons in High Definition?" Tripp asked as he crunched another spoonful of cereal.

"Yes," was all Joshua could muster until after the caffeine kicked in.

"I don't. These old MGM classics were shot on thirty-five millimeter film and shown in theaters. They had more definition than the stuff we watched as kids in the eighties."

Whatever. He was not that into film, unlike Tripp, who was a communications major and had movie posters all over the walls of their shared apartment in college. Tripp and his film buddies would get together some weekends and watch old black and white films Joshua had never heard of and then endlessly debate with each other, which was the best movie of all time, *Blade Runner* or *Citizen Kane*. Joshua called them all nerds and retreated to his room to hack on code.

Tripp was a Director for a local TV affiliate and his buddies were either washing dishes at some dive or had moved on to California to wait tables and debate about which version of *Blade Runner* was better; the original with a voice over or the director's cut with the new ending. Either way, they were not making a decent living and not making movies like they had hoped. Tripp still liked to watch movies and most of the time he watched them at Joshua's place. Tripp was the one who told Joshua which high definition TV to buy so they could have the best home theater that Joshua could afford.

"Hey, did you know that dude that died at RegTech yesterday?" Tripp asked.

"I was the one who found him."

"No shit? Man, I bet that was messed up."

Joshua was still not ready to rehash the day's events.

"They think he had a heart attack and died in his chair. He was not a picture of health like you and me," Joshua said poking fun at his friend's flab. In college they were on the tennis team and ran five miles a day. But lately they had become lazy and more prone to drinking beer and just skipping the whole exercising ordeal.

"Oh, I saw Delta Charlie this morning. She told me to tell you to check your IM for something." He was referring to Dancia. In high school Tripp and Joshua used to place labels on people who fit certain stereotypes so they could point them out in public and not be accused of "labeling" anyone, because that was not politically correct. The girls who wore black all the time were called Death Chicks and Tripp's unimaginative code word for them was Delta Charlie.

"Thanks," Joshua said, shaking off the afghan and taking his coffee with him as he went into the computer room.

"And take a shower. You stink man," Tripp called out after him.

Joshua sniffed himself as he sat down at the computer. Yep, he smelled like yesterday's laundry. Touching the mouse produced a login and he slowly pecked his password into the keyboard twice before being let into the system. The coffee had still not kicked in. He sat back and took a long drought of the miracle java with a soft, satisfying sigh. Tripp could still make a mean pot of coffee.

When his desktop came up he launched Pidgin, his instant messenger client and was soon staring at a message from Dancia. He rubbed the sand out of the corners of his eyes and tried to focus on the tiny font.

(05:15:35) Dancia Rivers: Check your XChat logs for last night on #coders. Looks like the Stuttgart police are calling Zemo's death a murder based on what his friends found on his computer the night he died. It was something about a message in his code. I looked in our CVS and it still had his code checked out. Guess we'll loose that change. Maybe I'm just morbid but I wonder what the code Glenn was working on looks like? I'll be by later. Thanks for letting me use your system last night. I finished the data layer and checked it into CVS. Laters.

They were working on an Open Source project that Joshua had started in college and had decided to resurrect. It was a movie rating and discussion web site, called MyMovies that he had built for Tripp and his film friends. They were updating the basic framework and redesigning it to make it "Web 2.0" and trendy so as to attract hardcore film geeks and maybe some investors. It was kind of like a cross between MySpace and the Internet Movie Database IMDB.

Joshua's leg started bouncing, the coffee was kicking in. His curiosity was piqued by what the German Police had found in Zemo's code. He logged into XChat, his Internet Relay Chat or IRC program, and then called up a terminal and started parsing through the logs in Vi, his code editor of choice, using regular expressions. Regular expressions were a kind of code shorthand for finding things in text documents. In just a few short minutes he had found the interesting part of last night's conversation between several of Zemo's friends.

In the middle of Zemo's code they found a calling card, a simple line that turned a freak death into murder. Buried in the code was a single sentence in English, "One down, three to go". There were no other messages in the code. No other files on his computer were touched. Someone had killed Zemo and wanted the crime to be noticed.

Joshua sat back in his chair, held his black coffee cup in his hands and took a slow drink. The similarity to Glenn's death disturbed him. Zemo's apparent cause of death was heart failure. No visible signs of struggle or self inflicted wounds. No family history of heart trouble, no history of illness or disease, just a perfectly healthy teenager dropping dead at his computer in the basement of his parents' house. Another tragic and sad death.

Joshua knew what Zemo's parents were going through, at least in some small way. He felt sorry for them and he felt sorry for Zemo. He was a bright kid and a gifted coder, the kind of talent that one rarely found these days in kids his age. He was well respected in the Open Source community too. Already there were Internet effigies being posted all around the globe. Forums and message boards were alive with talk about the murder and about who could possibly have done it, not to mention how they pulled it off.

Joshua scanned the web and quickly took in all the chatter about Zemo. He read forums, news sites and Digg stories all connected in some way to Zemo's death. The most interesting comment he read was from a well-respected member of the Free Software movement who wondered if the killer was in some twisted way, pulling off the ultimate hack.

Interesting. The notion that a hacker would seek attention and notoriety for the taking of another's life repulsed him, yet somehow fascinated him at the same time. It was not a very hacker-ish thing to do. The common press had bastardized the word hacker long ago as someone who played pranks on or otherwise caused harm to come to other people's computer systems. The true meaning of the word hacker was closer to a grand master of a trade. Someone who was so skilled in computers that there was little they could not make them do. Joshua had never met a true hacker. He knew some pretty gifted coders but they were either too immature or their egos were too large to truly be considered a hacker. If this murder was the work of a hacker he must surely be psychotic.

Joshua tilted his empty coffee mug and decided he needed a second cup. He padded back into the kitchen and noticed that Tripp had moved on to the news. More death and suffering from the Middle East flashed across the screen in bloody detail.

"I thought you were in the shower?" Tripp asked.

"I was reading some posts about Zemo, a coder in Germany who was murdered," Joshua said, pouring the last cup of coffee.

"What's with all the dead geeks? It must be a former jock getting his revenge," Tripp laughed at his comment.

"They're not related at least as far as I know." Joshua paused a moment wondering what might be embedded in Glenn's code. He did not notice anything yesterday when he checked in the code to source control. Program code was routinely stored in repositories known as source control, so that changes made to the code could easily be redacted. But then he never actually looked at Glenn's code. *Was there a secret message in his code too? Was Glenn a murder victim?*

Joshua headed back to the computer room taking a large sip from his mug. *Why would there be anything suspicious in Glenn's code?* Glenn was far from the talented coder that Zemo was. Maybe Joshua was letting his imagination get the best of him. Still, there was no way to be sure until he checked the code. Perhaps Dancia's hunch was right.

It only took him a few secure shell commands to get inside the RegTech firewall and start accessing the source control software. First he looked at the check-in times for all of the code that Glenn had checked out. When a programmer made changes to his code, he then checked the code into the repository. There were no more checkouts since Friday afternoon, when Joshua checked in Glenn's code. Next he checked out of the code repository all of Glenn's C Sharp code files. C Sharp was a programming language that they used at work. Using regular expressions again he was able to search for the words "One down" and in seconds, he had an answer - nothing. There were no matches for "One down, three to go" or even any word followed by "down".

Joshua breathed a sigh of relief. Then he started noticing the names of the code files in Glenn's repository. Everything seemed right except for the two files with a different extension. All C Sharp files ended in a *.cs* extension, but there were two files in the repository with a *.rb* extension. Those were written in the Ruby language. In all his conversations with Glenn about coding, Joshua had never heard the man mention anything positive about Ruby. Programmers love to compare coding languages like theologians compare religions. But in the end, most programmers specialize in only one language. Their support for that language often takes on a religious zeal.

Glenn was always a C Sharp proponent. He never gave any other language the time of day with the possible exception of Visual Basic the "other" Microsoft language. For him to have two Ruby language files in his project was like finding a crucifix in a Jewish Rabbi's house. Joshua remembered the last conversation they had about Ruby. Glenn had argued that it was just a passing fad and would never have the corporate support that a VB or a C Sharp would have. *Come to think of it, Glenn never actually dissed the language, only the acceptance of it.*

Joshua checked out one of the Ruby files and started scanning it looking more at the comments than the actual code. It was some kind of a C Sharp to Ruby conversion program, which meant that Glenn must have been working on ways to use C Sharp code in Ruby applications.

"Wow," Joshua said aloud.

He never realized that Glenn was a closet Ruby coder. It was hard to get his head around that idea. The program was a scratch script, something Glenn was using to try out some new ideas. It was not formal code used in an actual application.

There were very little comments and what was commented usually had things like "hope this works" or "change this later". The temporary notes were for him and did nothing to explain what was actually going on, which was the point of properly commented code.

Joshua opened the second file. It was a real source code file with a proper heading and was properly commented. Joshua recognized it immediately because he himself had written it. It was one of the models used in the MyMovies web application. He had co-written the model with the third member of their team named Themis. *So how the hell did Glenn get a copy of my code? Especially code that you had to pull from a closed repository for the MyMovies application? Could Themis have given it to him? I certainly didn't give it to him.*

It made no sense, unless Glenn was Themis. The thought lingered in his mind until it crystallized. *Was Glenn the third member of their MyMovies team? How could that be?* Then Joshua realized that he really knew very little about Themis. They had conversed on IRC quite a bit over the past few months but they had talked mostly about Ruby and how to construct Ruby web applications. Neither one had mentioned what they did for a living, only that they loved Ruby and wanted to work on a project together. Themis was brought onto the MyMovies team because Joshua invited him. Dancia didn't know who he was either, but at the time, she agreed they needed his expertise. They all knew who Zemo was and Zemo knew who they were, but nobody knew the real identity of Themis. Since everyone on the project referred to each other by their hacker alias, it was doubtful that Themis even knew who they were. Such was the way things were on the net.

As he looked at the code he and Themis had written he noticed the message plain as day -- "Two down, two to go". The killer had left his calling card in the code of two members of Joshua's web application team. *Someone is targeting us! How long before Dancia and I am attacked?*

Did either of them notice the line before they died? Then he realized just how insane the idea of killing someone sitting at their computer was. *How could you kill with code? Was the sentence a trigger for another program to run or was it just a signature card and nothing else? I have to find out.*

He logged into Glenn's computer to see if it had been the victim of a root kit. Root kits were back door programs that Black Hat Crackers left on computers that had been compromised. A good root kit would let the bad guy into the computer at any time and have his full way with all the vital system files, essentially running as the machine's administrator.

Joshua knew about root kits but he was not an expert in finding them. For that he would need some help from a security expert, someone trained in the black art of cracking into computers for the sole purpose of catching those who did such things without consent. *I need Psycho.* Psycho was the handle of a talented security admin that Joshua knew from college. His real name was Nik Sikes, but everyone called him Psycho because when it came to doing what he did, Sikes was just plain crazy. Psycho was a freelance security expert, hired by companies to break into their systems and find their weaknesses. He would sneak into every computer on a network and drive the company's security expert's nuts trying to catch him.

It was a valuable skill to have in these times of complete reliance on computers and networks. Sikes made obscene money doing what he did and traveled the world doing it. Every time he was back in Boise to catch up on his snail mail, Joshua would hook up with him and they'd go out drinking together. Sikes always had some entertaining stories to tell about how he was able to break into some big client's system and they never knew he was there. One time he was able to catch a Black Hatter at his own game by laying a trap for him. When the client flew him out to their offices in Singapore, Sikes had already been through their networks and caught the offending cracker in his tracks. All he had to do was show them what he had done and accept his fat paycheck.

Joshua knew he had to chat with Sikes but he didn't know where in the world his friend was working. That was what IRC was so good for. He logged onto his favorite channel and checked who was online. Sure enough, there was Psycho. A quick ping to see if he was actually at the computer came up empty. Even people who spent the majority of their lives on a computer were away from the keyboard sometimes.

CHAPTER 3

IT WAS A LITTLE before noon on Sunday when Joshua finally found Psycho on IRC. Tripp had gotten bored and went home muttering something about going to the movies with one of his film friends. Joshua hadn't told him about the connection between Glenn and Zemo. He knew that Tripp would insist on telling the police and Joshua was not ready to go there yet.

Joshua was on his computer searching message boards for information on Zemo. The blogosphere was running out of ideas about who killed the German teenager. The consensus seemed to be that it was someone in the community but nobody could agree on who it might be. Joshua was beginning to realize that he might be in a unique position to find out who killed Zemo and Glenn. The Boise Police were unaware of the damning message he found in Glenn's code and thus probably were none the wiser for it. If he could just get into Glenn's system and look around, who knew where that might lead him. Back in the chat room, Joshua began typing to his friend. He didn't normally use an alias while on IRC unless he wanted anonymity.

<jjones>   Psycho, where are you?
<psycho>   City of Trees, my friend.   I just got in from
             Tokyo yesterday.
<jjones>   Can I buy you lunch? I want to pick your
             brain.
<psycho>   Sure man. Bar Gernika?

<jjones>   I'll pick you up in few.

<psycho>   Just come on in, door's unlocked.

Joshua smiled to himself; only Psycho would leave his doors unlocked in the real world and live inside Fort Knox in the cyber world.

Sikes lived in an older East Side subdivision situated just under Boise's Bench and protected by the sun for much of the year. Large shade trees and expensive, older homes where close-knit neighborhoods kept each other in line with restrictive covenants, dominated the area. It was some of the prettiest tree lined real estate in Boise. Many of the housing developments surrounding the city were either carved out of the desert or paved over farmland. Next to the trendy North End, it was one of the nicest communities to live in.

Joshua pulled over and parked his silver Porsche in front of the house. At least his car looked like it belonged there. As he walked across the yard to the front door, he noticed the front windows were all cracked open. It was a pleasant forty-eight degrees and the snow was already melting from the previous day's storm. Joshua tried the door and it was indeed unlocked, in fact it was cracked open just like the windows.

Once inside, he stepped gingerly over a meshwork of LAN cables and power cords leading to the living room. Every spare inch of floor space was covered with various computer cases and odd printers. There was no place to sit and barely enough room to walk around them. The house was humming with the fan noise and it was noticeably warmer inside than outside. *Must be nice to be able to afford such gratuitous power consumption.*

"Sikes?"

"Back here man!" Sikes hollered from deep inside the house.

Joshua walked back toward the bedrooms past the living area and the kitchen. Every room was crammed with humming PCs, including a few on the kitchen counters. He found Sikes in the spare bedroom hunched over an open PC case in the process of swapping out a power supply. He was dressed in a pair of old army fatigues with side pockets and wore a faded red T-shirt with black kanji script on it and no shoes. His red hair was tucked under a pirate bandanna and ran down below his shoulders. He wore a long goatee that naturally curled upward making him look like a tall Munchkin from the Wizard of Oz.

"Just firing up the matrix here, be done in a few."

The "matrix" was what he called his network of computers running every flavor of operating system under the sun, including a Sun Solaris Sparc station. He used them to practice breaking into networks composed of every kind of computer imaginable. Some of them were identical units with nothing more than a different version of an operating system on them so he could replicate un-patched and patched systems. Others were just oddball configurations that he had ran across and replicated just for the experience.

Security gurus tend to become very intimate with the operating systems they specialized in. They can describe the inner workings of the hardware and how the software makes calls to the hardware. Only those who actually design operating systems know more about low-level operations.

"This old Windows 98 box blew a drive while I was gone. She gave up the ghost and nearly caught fire," Sikes said, as he replaced the cover to the CPU case and stood up. He offered a quick hand shake to Joshua.

"Good to see you again, what's on your mind?"

"Murder."

Sikes lifted his left eyebrow in a perfect imitation of Spock from TV's Star Trek.

Joshua waited for him to slip on his hiking boots before they left. In the Porsche on the way downtown, he outlined what he knew about Glenn and Zemo's deaths. Sikes listened intently and stared off into traffic to ponder the ramifications.

"Wasn't Zemo one of Captain America's villains?" asked

Sikes.

"I didn't read comics."

Sikes looked at Joshua like he was crazy, then he shook his head and mumbled.

"He was a German scientist and founder of the Masters of Evil. Dude, Zemo invented the Death Ray or," Sikes put up finger quotes, "Laser Beam", imitating Doctor Evil from Austin Powers, "years before anyone else had them."

Joshua nodded politely thinking his friend must not be all there. He wondered if comic book geeks actually believed the story lines or if they were just so into the imaginary universes that it only seemed like they did to outsiders. He supposed it was not too different from Tripp and his friends quoting movie lines and talking about movie characters like they were real people.

"Well, this Zemo was a damn good coder and his death is a loss for this world."

Sikes nodded in agreement.

"I didn't know the kid, but I like his sense of style in picking such a cool and well thoughtout alias. Most people just use the names of fictional characters that everyone is familiar with."

Joshua agreed with his friend, Zemo was definitely an original.

Bar Gernika was a hole in the wall joint just off Capital Boulevard in down town Boise. One of the most popular Basque restaurants in town, the impossibly small establishment was nearly dead on this clear November day. Joshua parked in the Bank of America parking lot next door and they walked around the corner to the entrance of the bar.

Joshua set his laptop on the table away from where they would be served. A tall, thin man dressed in a black punk rock T-shirt and black jeans appeared. Joshua ordered a lamb grinder with pepper jack cheese and a beer. Sikes ordered the same thing minus the pepper jack.

"Tell me how a Windows system could be compromised?"

Sikes laughed.

"Let me count the ways."

"Okay, how about one inside a corporate firewall?"

"Tougher, but not impossible. You would want to look for some way through the firewall, be it a server port or an FTP port, IRC, that kind of thing. Once you can get to the target PC, its fair game. Most big business computers are kept up to date on patches, but Microsoft only publishes fixes for about half the exploits found in the wild. If you had knowledge of any one of those exploits, you're in like Flynn."

Joshua nodded.

"So the bad guy would have to know about Windows exploits in order to get in?"

"Not necessarily, he could just be using a program designed by a more experienced programmer. You know, like script kiddies. Kids who don't have a clue how it was written use most of the malicious software out there. Some clever coder figures out a way to get into a system and then writes a brilliant program that makes it easy for other, less knowledgeable people to use and abuse. That's how Denial of Service programs thrive."

Joshua stared with a furrowed brow at an old rusted farm implement on the wall collecting his thoughts. "So I guess I need to know how you could take remote control of a PC and not be noticed by a user."

"Ah, what you would use for that is..." Sikes lowered his voice as if he didn't want anyone within earshot to hear him. He leaned forward and then looked around the nearly deserted bar. There were two older women at a table about ten feet away absorbed in idle conversation about their gardens. He motioned for Joshua to lean forward and then whispered.

"...a root kit."

"What?" Joshua said.

Sikes started laughing out loud as if he just told the best joke ever. Joshua smiled to cover his confusion there was nothing secret about root kits. Psycho was just nutty.

"Seriously, dude. Lighten up. This is how I make a living."

"Sorry man I'm just trying to find out who killed some people I know. I feel like I owe it to them."

Sikes sat back and wiped the smile off of his reddish face. The waiter returned with their drinks and sandwiches. They both dug in and the table fell silent for a few minutes as they enjoyed their meal. Sikes ate fast as if he were not used to letting nourishment get in his way of working. He finished his beer and his sandwich and then toyed with his fries.

"Most Black Hatters use a kernel level root kit. Although there are plenty of people using application and library level kits, they tend to be much easier to detect. Believe it or not, it's not very common to find root kits on Windows boxes, especially the kernel level ones. If that's what you have, it's usually the mark of a serious bad boy."

Joshua finished chewing and swallowed. "I don't really know what's on Glenn's box. Is there any way to detect a root kit?"

Sikes slouched back in his chair, shoved a fry into his mouth and chewed slowly.

"His PC is inside the RegTech firewall and it probably has a virus scanner on it that is kept up-to-date by the site IT. Higher-level root kits are out of the question. He has to have a kernel level job, a program that runs in the actual operating system. In that case the best way to check for it is to boot his machine into safe mode and then check it for unusual processes. You might get lucky.

"You see, what makes a root kit so hard to detect is that it's loaded into the kernel as a device driver and once it's in there it can act as a interceptor for all incoming calls to the kernel and redirect scans to discover it. Virus protection software companies hate them."

Joshua finished his sandwich and pushed the basket aside. He took out his laptop and opened it up. There was a wireless hot spot nearby. He opened a terminal and securely connected to Glenn's computer at RegTech under his own user name. Then he slid the laptop across to Sikes.

"Can you find anything just by poking around?"

Sikes sat up and pulled the silver MacBook Pro closer to him. He cracked his slender fingers and then started typing like a master pianist. Joshua moved his chair around beside Sikes so he could see what he was doing. The waiter came by again and cleared their baskets. He asked them if they wanted more beers and Joshua motioned for two more. The guy nodded, indifferent to their interest in the laptop and nearly indifferent to them.

"He's got an open port using SSH. It looks like it goes to a directory on another computer. Your boy was probably streaming MP3's from his home."

"I think he mentioned that he had set up something like that. He was boasting about subverting the site IT because they couldn't see what he was streaming through Secure Shell. They don't allow streaming media at RegTech."

Sikes nodded, his fingers had moved on to other directories. "Mmmm, this is interesting. He was using mIRC a popular Windows IRC client. You should snag his logs, might help you find his killer."

"I was going to get those if I could log in as him or get admin rights to his box."

"Looks like all the common ports are blocked as per corporate IT procedures. He was running Internet Information Services, but only as localhost."

"We're a web team; we all run that to test our development code." Sikes made a gag face, and Joshua shrugged. Microsoft's web server was not well liked by security professionals. It was a constant source of security break-ins.

"It's not possible to really know if this box is owned unless you have physical access, but just from what I've seen, I'd say it was a kernel level hack. Which means your killer knew what he was doing. If that's the case, he still has access to this box and he's still in control of it."

Sikes logged out of the SSH terminal and sat back again in thought. Joshua moved the laptop back to his side of the table and closed it down.

"I'd be amazed if he left the mIRC client logs in place. This guy has full control of this box. He could wipe all evidence away and nobody would be the wiser."

"Maybe he thought IT would just reformat the hard drive and everything would be taken care of for him?"

Sikes shook his head. "These Cracker types are just like thieves. They are paranoid beyond belief. They have to be. If they leave anything at all behind, guys like me can catch them. That's why the best ones are never found, until they slip up."

"What do you think I should do with his box then?"

"Boot it into safe mode, start checking for processes that you can't identify or that should not be there. There's a page on my web site that lists all the processes running on a stock Windows XP Pro install. You can use that as a baseline to start from. Of course your IT will have anti-virus stuff on there and maybe some programs to push patches and stuff. Then you have to do an inventory of what crazy stuff he installed like shareware apps and open source programs. It could take you a while."

Joshua grinned sheepishly.

"What else would I be doing on a Saturday night?"

CHAPTER 4

DETECTIVE BILL PLAIT pulled in behind the police cruiser and parked his late model Buick. He looked around briefly to assess the quiet residential neighborhood in West Boise. It was the kind of charming, tree-lined street where nothing bad ever happened. On this day, the violence had come to the suburbs.

As he walked up the front walk he was approached by Officer Samantha Nelson; a stout policewoman with a solid stance and a pleasant, round face.

"What do we have Sam?"

"Henry Levine, a white, elderly male, maybe in his seventies, shot in the head, execution style. No signs of a struggle and nothing out of place, as least as far as we can tell."

They walked into the open garage and Plait immediately noticed the clutter. It was hard to miss. There were shelves of technical books all the way to the ceiling along the far wall of the garage. The two remaining walls were filled with drawers and cabinets that were overstuffed with electronics and parted out radios. It was the kind of junky garage that kids loved to explore and wives were ashamed of.

Lying on the dirty concrete floor was the victim. He was facing down, a small entry wound at the back of his balding head. There was enough gray matter and other fleshy parts on the floor to make looking at the exit wound unnecessary.

Plait looked around at the desks built into the wall of the

garage. There were Ham radios stacked on wooden shelves and lots of paper logbooks. Everything looked like it was well used and well loved by its owner. Various test instruments surrounded a workbench that had the guts of a radio spread out like a large filleted fish.

"He must have been a radio hobbyist or something," Nelson said, looking around the garage in amusement.

"They call them Hams, I believe. Who reported the body?" Plait asked.

"Lady next door, she was out in her back yard when she heard a shot and a car pulling away."

Plait looked up at Officer Nelson.

"She didn't get an ID on the car, sir. She came back inside and called 911."

"Is there anyone else in the house? Relatives, spouse?"

"No sir, apparently he was a bachelor. The neighbor lady is waiting if you'd like to question her?"

Plait nodded. Whoever the man upset, he was pretty hard core, there was powder burns on the dead man's head, indicating the killer was standing right beside him.

"This is Detective Plait, Mrs. Zigler. He's investigating the murder," Officer Nelson explained.

Mrs. Zigler was in her eighties and wore a polyester flower print dress and a knit sweater. She was sitting in her front parlor where she spent a good deal of her time, watching the traffic pass. She was a little hard of hearing and Officer Nelson spoke loud enough so she could hear her.

"Good afternoon, Mrs. Zigler, I understand you heard a gun shot this afternoon?"

The woman slowly nodded. She was visibly upset by the day's events and kept shaking her head.

"Yes, I was out in the back yard with Muffin. She was doing her business and I was putting sunflower seeds in my bird feeder."

Plait took a knee before the woman and wrote notes in his wire bound notepad.

"Do you remember what time it was?"

"Why yes, I do. I always put Muffin out at three in the afternoon. Today was no different."

Plait looked up at Nelson who was smiling. Sometimes luck was on their side, other times it was not. He jotted down the time.

"Did you hear any voices coming from Mr. Levine's home while you and Muffin were outside?"

She furled her brow and looked at him astonished.

"No, I can't say that I did. Got hearing aides you know."

Plait smiled at the woman who honestly thought he was a little slow.

"Mrs. Zigler, did Mr. Levine have many visitors in the last week, as far as you know?"

She glanced out the window and watched a car pass by. "He doesn't get many visitors at all these days. Margaret died oh, about two years ago now. He mostly just stays in his garage and fiddles with those old radios of his."

Plait looked around her dining room. The furniture was from the nineteen sixties and so was the decor. Muffin was sitting on a cushion seat nearby, a small white poodle. An ambulance pulled in next-door and the dog's ears perked up and she moved over to look out the low main windows. The dog stood tall enough to see clearly over the windowsill.

"Does Muffin notice when she sees Mr. Levine's car come home?"

"Oh yes, we keep a pretty good eye on the neighborhood, Muffin and I," she said, petting the poodle on the head.

Detective Plait stood up and thanked the old woman for her time. They only told her that her neighbor had been shot, they did not explain how for fear of upsetting her further. Perhaps a detailed study of Mr. Levine's personal records would turn up something.

Back inside the old man's house, Plait went over items on the desk in the den. It was where Henry paid his bills. There was an old PC that looked like it was purchased over a decade ago. He picked up some of the papers on the desk and skimmed through them, bills mostly. He was looking for some kind of documentation that would indicate any sort of criminal activity.

He nudged the mouse of the computer by accident and it snapped the monitor to life. On the screen was a web browser opened to Craig's List, a popular on-line classified site where you could buy and sell things to people directly. He looked closer at the item on the screen. It was registered to Henry Levine and it was some kind of electronic device. Plait got out his glasses and put them on so he could read the tiny print on the screen.

It was a cell-phone jamming device of some kind. Henry was disappointed with the device and was looking to unload it at a fair price. There were no takers for the item, not even a comment; the site was pretty bare bones. *Damn, that would have been too easy.* Then he thought about email, Craig's List customers primarily emailed each other about sales. He opened Outlook Express and scanned the latest emails for cell phone jammers. Nothing.

There was another Ham radio on the desk, a hand held model that was still on. He picked it up and thought about it for a second, maybe the killer was a Ham and they met on the air. Plait wrote down the frequency number displayed on the face of the little Yaesu handy talkie. He knew a Ham back at the precinct that may be able to tell him what the number meant.

CHAPTER 5

JOSHUA DROPPED PSYCHO off at his house and pointed the shiny silver car toward the west side of town. As he pulled into the parking lot at RegTech, he flashed his security badge at the guard who waved his car in with a bored look of someone who did not want to be at work. Joshua had the car's top down and he wore a heavy brown cotton overcoat to insulate him from the chilled air. Black Wayfarer sunglasses protected his eyes from the bright sunshine and framed his unkempt collar length hair. Brown leather driving gloves helped him keep a good grip on the smooth wheel of the little sports car.

Joshua's father had been a life long Porsche aficionado and had owned half dozen different types for as far back as Joshua could remember. Before the accident that took his life, John Jones had owned a sterling silver 1958 Porsche 356 Convertible D. He doted over it more than anything else he owned. Joshua associated the friendly, round head lamps with his father's warm personality, and could not bring himself to sell the little convertible. The elegant sports car turned heads all the time despite being old enough for classic car plates.

Joshua drove the convertible until the bitter cold of winter completely froze him out. Then he had it cleaned up, tuned and put back into the garage. He didn't care so much about the elements but he was careful to keep the car clean and in good running order. He was not mechanically inclined himself but he was well off enough to make sure that only confident and certified Porsche mechanics ever touched his baby. In that respect he was very much like his father. He even attended road rallies and Porsche drive-ins across the western states where the same car nuts that knew his father got together to talk sports cars and drink German beer. None of that could stop the feelings of guilt from creeping up on him, but it did give Joshua some solace.

Joshua noticed several cars in the parking lot; not everyone took the weekend off. He pulled the Porsche into an empty spot near the closest entrance and got out. Reaching into what constituted a back seat he pulled out the cloth satchel containing his laptop and headed for the entrance. There was no sign of anyone in building four. The lights were again in energy saver mode and flickered on as he headed for Glenn's cube.

Joshua sat down at Glenn's PC. He needed to be logged on as Glenn or administrator for what he wanted to do. He knew Glenn hated having to log into his computer so he somehow doubted that the programmer wasted much time remembering a new password every ninety days. He pulled out the ergonomic keyboard and looked underneath it for a password written on the bottom. It was blank. He looked around carefully at the sparse furnishings. Just a coaster made from some kind of rock and a few pages of program specs. There was a black stapler and a plastic cup penholder with one cheap pen and a well-chewed pencil. Some paper clips lay at the bottom of the cup. The garbage and wrappers from all of his junk food were gone.

Joshua pulled open a desk drawer and found it filled with unopened candy bars and bags of chips. It looked like Glenn did his shopping at one of those cost savings warehouses and bought it in bulk. Smart, considering how often he ate the stuff. Joshua often had to scrounge around pretty hard to come up with sixty-five cents for a Coke at his desk. Something caused him to reach down under the low-slung Herman Miller chair where he found a sticky note taped to the chair's frame. Bingo. His password was nothing unusual, just a random string of characters auto generated by the IT department. They gave up running password breaking software just to find simple passwords like dog's names or movie star names in favor of generating their own passwords and making the user remember whatever crazy combination they drew by chance. Joshua figured they had several dozen calls a day for resetting passwords.

He typed in the random characters and waited for the operating system to boot up. He started Outlook and checked to see if Glenn had received any postmortem emails. He had but they were mostly internal company group mailings reaching hundreds of employees. The list barely changed when people left the group or the company. There was nothing suspicious in the email. He closed the email program and checked the Start menu for mIRC.

After the IRC client auto-logged into several channels Joshua took note of them in a small tablet he kept in his coat pocket. He loitered for a few minutes. There didn't seem to be anything unusual going on. Joshua took the time to write down all the user names in the smaller channels. Some of them had hundreds of members on-line and he didn't bother with them.

Next came the inventory of all the programs Glenn had added since his machine's last re-imaging. A re-image occurred when the operating system was installed again to get a clean new system. There were surprisingly few shareware or open source programs on his system. Glenn really wasn't a slacker when at work. He spent most of his time programming. There were things like Google Earth and some Free Software for network packet sniffing, nothing too unusual. Joshua recognized the media player he used as being written by a programmer in another building - GAmp. It had an extensive playlist when Joshua brought it up. He saved the information to a pen drive that he had in his coat pocket. Most of the songs on the playlist were not on his work computer. There was a SSH tunnel that Joshua remembered Glenn had mentioned. As Joshua poked around he found a Visual Basic Script that launched the connection. Glenn sure hadn't made it hard to find that one.

Joshua thought about playing some of the music and then he looked at Glenn's padded Sony headphones and realized that the last person to wear them was a corpse. Perhaps not.

Finding the program's process was going to take a while so he decided to go get some coffee. He snagged his cup from his cube and headed off down the hall towards the coffee station. He had the distinct feeling of *déjà-vu* as he started making a fresh pot of coffee. He slowly walked back to Glenn's cube thinking about Friday and how Glenn and Zemo's deaths had given him a new mission in life and a new respect for how fragile life can be.

Some movement caught his eye and he noticed another programmer was present. Peering over the cubicles he saw Lawrence Taggert coming in and entering his cubical. Larry was the only UNIX programmer in the web group. He did the administration of the Linux boxes they used as file servers and any scripting that was needed. He was an old school programmer, had been coding longer than anyone else on the team. Joshua remembered that Larry used to work with his father back in the seventies. The guy hardly ever talked to anyone. Joshua didn't really know much about him personally but he knew he didn't use Windows and he ran his Linux box in terminal mode. Which was pretty hard core. Whenever Joshua had a question about Linux he would ask Larry and always got a concise and short answer with little or no commentary. Larry was all business and kept to himself any details of his private life. Joshua could respect that about him and never tried to be his buddy. Even now when they were the only two people in the building Joshua would not think to bother him.

Joshua sat down at Glenn's PC and got to work. A couple of hour's worth of investigating further and he was sure that he had accounted for all the processes running on Glenn's computer. He did a reboot into safe mode like Sikes had suggested and looked for anything out of place. It looked clean. Either the root kit was harder to find or it was removed. Somehow he felt like he was missing something. Then it dawned on him - the music hack. *Could the bad guy have come in through that connection from Glenn's home computer? If so then his work PC was just a conduit. Sneaky, very sneaky.* He looked around at Glenn's cube and realized there was nothing more to do. He logged off and went back to his cube. He propped up his feet on his desk and slowly finished his cup of coffee.

A picture began to form in his mind about what had happened to Glenn. His home PC was hacked into and the killer used the SSH connection to the work PC to somehow get to Glenn. How exactly he was able to kill Glenn was still not clear. Joshua wondered if Zemo was compromised in a similar fashion. He briefly pondered if there was a friend in Stuttgart who was trying to work out who killed Zemo. More likely it was a computer crimes expert at the local police station or whatever they had in Germany. *Too bad they didn't publish what they knew about the Zemo case.* He dropped his feet from the desk and sat up. Maybe they didn't, but the city had a newspaper and he might be able to glean some details about the investigation by reading what they had published about the case.

He quickly logged onto his PC and googled for newspapers in Stuttgart Germany. He found three web sites for newspapers in the city and ran them through a web-based translator. One of them, Stuttgarter Zeitung, had a local Police report section and he found a fairly detailed account of Zemo's murder investigation. The translation was not perfect but good enough to get the gist of it.

Police had originally thought the death was of natural causes there were no signs of malice and no obvious motive. A friend of Zemo's from the local Stuttgart University had come by to pay his respects to the kid's family and wound up carting off all his computer gear. The parents never really approved of their son's hacking and they were happy to give away his gear not a day after his death. While that sounded cold, Joshua knew the parents were acting in emotional self-defense. Little did they know the move was going to take a bizarre twist. It was this college friend who had found the message in Zemo's code and alerted police. At that point a murder investigation was launched, and all of the computers used by Zemo were confiscated by the police as evidence.

Joshua realized that crucial evidence was out of his reach and that if he went to the local police about what he found on Glenn's PC he might very well lose what access he had to Glenn's computers. There was no guarantee that the Boise Police Department would ever be able to find out what he could simply by poking around. He knew that the best chance of finding out what happened to Glenn and possibly to Zemo lay with his own investigation. It was a challenge that he accepted without further thought or deliberation. He had too. It could mean his own life or even, God forbid, Dancia's life.

Joshua sent an email to the IT person he knew and requested that Glenn's computers be left untouched for at least a week while they made sure all the code he was working on was cleaned off. It was a legitimate request and he knew that Todd, the IT guy, would honor it. It would take management several weeks to hire a replacement or they could decide to distribute his work to the remaining programmers. *That would be typical for clueless managers.*

He glanced down and realized that it was getting late, which could have explained the growing hunger in his stomach. He logged off and gathered up his satchel. Chinese sounded good to him tonight and he knew that Dancia and her roommate, Trish, both loved Yen Ching's Chinese restaurant. He wondered briefly how Dancia would react when he told her what he had found.

CHAPTER 6

"BEWARE OF GEEKS bearing food," Joshua quipped as Trish let him in and took some bags from him. Joshua had shown up at Dancia and Trish's apartment with his arms full of Chinese take out boxes. Trish answered the door wearing a T-shirt and flannel pants, her face was all made up like she was getting ready for a date. Her blond hair was pulled back in a ponytail. She was naturally pretty with blue eyes and a slender build. Tripp had the hots for her but she was not Joshua's type. He preferred women who could hold an interesting conversation for longer than ten minutes without getting bored. Trish was cute and nice but not for him.

"Hello Joshua. Is this for us?"

He nodded as he looked around the small apartment.

"Is she up yet?"

"Of course not," Trish said, as she brought the food to the small round kitchen table.

"More for you and me then."

"Actually, I have a date tonight but thanks for thinking of me. You're so sweet," she said as she kissed him on the cheek. She glided past him and down the hall to rap on Dancia's bedroom door.

"Juliet, Romeo brought you some breakfast," Trish teased.

There were no signs of life from Dancia's room so she came back to the kitchen. "She'll be out when she smells the food.

Gosh it's making me hungry."

"So who's the lucky guy tonight?" Joshua asked as he opened some boxes and started separating the wooden chopsticks.

"Someone I met at the restaurant. Gary Summers, he's a lawyer I think," she said as if she thought that were a good thing. Joshua nodded and dug into the fried rice.

"What are you two up to tonight?" she said her tone suggestive as she wiped a loose strand of hair from her eyes.

Joshua finished chewing and swallowed. "Oh you know, writing some code, surfing the net, plotting world domination, the usual."

Trish laughed. "You two are pathetic. You should go to a movie or out dancing."

"We're just friends Trish, besides geeks don't dance."

She smiled. "Right. You've never seen Dancia cut loose to Techno music have you?"

Joshua stopped chewing and stared at Trish as he tried to imagine that. "No, I can't even picture that."

"She's pretty hot. You should see her dance some time." Trish glanced at the wall clock and stood up. "I have to get dressed Gary will be here soon. Excuse me." She headed for her room and closed the door.

Joshua helped himself to the Sweet and Sour Pork and looked around. Their apartment was clean and modestly appointed. It was smartly decorated in the way that only women could accomplish. It was definitely not a bachelor's pad. He knew that Trish was responsible for most of it because Dancia could care less about decorating. Her room was always messy and decorated with things like framed car ads from the 1950's and Jazz posters from the Boise Jazz Festival. Dancia was the Oscar and Trish the Felix of this odd paring.

Dancia's door opened and she came shuffling out down the hall wearing a sleep-shirt. She squinted in the kitchen light. "What are you doing here?" she asked as she moved to the couch and curled up in a ball. The smell of the pork and rice was permeating the small apartment and making her stomach growl. Her black hair was frumpy from sleep.

"I found out some interesting things today and you need to know about them."

She opened her dark eyes. "What things?"

Joshua got up and looked down the hallway. He could hear Trish's stereo playing music so he moved across the room to sit beside Dancia on the long couch. His voice was low just in case Trish overheard them.

"Glenn was actually Themis and he was murdered by the same guy who got Zemo."

"Glenn was Themis?"

She sat up, her white sleep-shirt tight against her chest. She wiped the sand out of one eye. "Really?"

"I found a message in his code at work. It was just like what they found in Zemo's code."

"Holy shit, we could be next!" she said, her eyes wide-awake.

Joshua nodded solemnly. They stared at each other for a moment each one realizing that they may be getting in over their heads.

"Damn. Have you gone to the police yet?" Dancia finally asked.

"No. I don't want to until I have a better idea who it was that killed him."

She pulled her legs up under her oversized white shirt and held her cold toes in her hands. "Good, the police would be clueless."

Joshua nodded in agreement with her.

"That's not all," he said.

"I spoke with Psycho at lunch. He showed me how to tell if Glenn's PC had been hacked. Turns out it was. He was streaming MP3's through a secure shell connection to his home

PC. It appears that the bad guy hacked his home box and came in through the open port."

"Sneaky," she said her eyes shinning.

Joshua took another bite of pork. "That's all I've got so far."

She got up and walked to the table adjusting her panties as she walked. Joshua pointed to the food on the table with his chopsticks. "I got you *Char siu* and some white rice."

"Thanks. You want something to drink?"

"What do you have?"

"Looks like Coke or water I'm afraid."

"Better make it Coke we could be in for a late night," Joshua said. He came back to the table for more fried rice.

Dancia brought him a cold can of Coke in a coozy and picked up her bucket of barbecue pork. They re-convened back on the couch.

"Did you find anything useful on Glenn's work PC?"

Joshua shook his head. "No, it was just the conduit. There were a few mIRC logs and some trivial programs that he added to his system, nothing directly responsible for anything."

"We can start going over his logs and try to find out who he was dealing with. Be better if we could get his home PC."

Joshua chewed on his meal and thought for a moment. "I wonder if we could sneak into his house and capture an image of his hard drive."

Dancia stopped chewing and looked at him. "Ah, that's breaking and entering. A crime last time I checked."

"Glenn was not big on security. It's possible he left a back door open or something."

Dancia continued eating. "Do you know where he lived?"

Joshua shook his head. "Somewhere on the East side I think. We can just google his name and get that."

Dancia nodded as she ate. There were an alarming number of things you could find out about someone by simply putting their full name into a search engine. Even without paying for a service if you knew what you were doing you could access hundreds of public documents, all of which held valuable information about whomever you were searching for.

Trish came out of her room dressed to the nines for her date. She did a fashion model twirl in front of Dancia and Joshua. "Well, how do I look my peeps?"

Joshua did a geeky imitation of a catcall whistle. Dancia eyeballed her roommate from head to toe in a very precise, critical manner that only another woman could provide. "Those shoes don't work with that dress. Get your black boots."

Trish looked down at her feet and frowned. "I broke the heel on them last week. This is all I have that even half matches."

Dancia waved it off. "Never mind you look fine then."

Joshua nodded in agreement. "I think you look great Trish. Gary will love it. When will he be here?"

"Any minute. Damn that Chinese food smells good." She walked over to the table and checked out what they were eating.

"We have reservations at the Game Keeper."

Dancia and Joshua exchanged looks. The Game Keeper was an upscale restaurant downtown.

"Must be a law partner," Dancia said.

"Yeah pretty impressive catch."

Trish turned around and came over in front of the couch. "He's a bit older than I usually date but Gary has style, you know?"

"And lots of mullah," Dancia grinned.

Trish shrugged with a sly smile. "You can't blame a girl for trying."

Trish glided over to answer the ringing doorbell. Gary was a short, dignified man who looked to be in his late forties. His dark hair was thinning and he wore a slick mustache. Dancia didn't care for him right off the bat but she pretended to be impressed. Trish grabbed her purse at the door and went outside with a quick look over her shoulder. Joshua gave her thumbs up and Dancia was locked in a forced smile of approval.

As soon as the door shut, Dancia wiped the smile off her face. "She's crazy. That guy's a slime ball." Joshua nodded in agreement. She got up and moved to the front window to peek out at them. She watched Gary help Trish into his Cadillac CTS and then he walked around the back of it to get in himself. He moved with a swaying motion that reminded her of a mobster from Brooklyn. As they drove away she turned around and headed for her bedroom. "I'm getting a shower. You can use my computer to look up his address then we can take a drive out to see his house."

Joshua followed her down the hall to the master bedroom. Dancia was a night shift worker and her bedroom was modified to accommodate her lifestyle. There were cardboard baffles around her door on the inside to keep out daylight. Her window was covered with cardboard boxes and duct tape. She had curtains covering the window but they were as plain as the rest of her decor. The first thing Joshua noticed was the pile of clothes all over her floor. Dancia was a slob and she made no effort to hide it or apologize for it, especially in her own room.

She had a dresser and the several drawers that were open contained presumably clean clothes. But no real effort had been made to fold them and they fell out onto the floor like overflowing water from a glass. Her bed had a white down comforter on it and a sheet wrapped up underneath it. Several fluffy pillows were strewn about near the head of the bed. She liked candles and there were several still burning as they entered the room. *I wonder if the scented candles are masking other funk,* Joshua thought.

He smiled to himself as he waded over to her computer/ makeup desk. She had a new Mac Pro complete with a wireless Mac mouse and keyboard. Some slender Mac style speakers surrounded her 24-inch cinema flat panel monitor. It was on so all he had to do was switch to his own login.

Dancia grabbed some underwear from her dresser and headed into the bathroom. He could hear the water running as if she had not closed the door. He started to think about what that meant when he caught himself and focused on his task at hand. He brought up a browser and searched for, "Glenn Becker + Boise + Idaho". After a few false starts he quickly found his former co-worker's address. He was right. Glenn had lived on the East side near the Simplot Sports Complex.

He looked around the desk for a printer and didn't find one. So he searched for a scrap of paper and a pen. There were some bills laid out on the desk but no loose paper. He pushed his fingers around under the makeup cases and found a pen. She had some colored sticky notes tacked to her monitor - reminders of when to pay bills and few phone numbers that he didn't recognize. There were no drawers in the desk unit so he dug in her wastebasket for an old envelope. He scribbled the address, folded the envelope and stuck it in his pocket.

While he was waiting for Dancia to finish her shower he scanned the latest posts to Slashdot and Digg, two technology related discussion sites, to see if anyone had learned anything else about Zemo's killer. There were some interesting posts but nothing related to Zemo or Glenn. He was reading an article on out-sourcing IT workers from the local newspaper when she came out of the bathroom. She had a towel tucked under her arms as she fumbled around the darkened room, looking for an outfit.

"I found his address, do you want me to wait outside?" Joshua asked.

"No, you're fine. I just have to find a bra. Oh, the laundry room," she said turning down the hall.

Joshua was a little uncomfortable with being in her room while she was trying to get dressed. It was every boy's dream to be in the same bedroom as a girl who was getting dressed but he somehow never really thought of Dancia in that way, at least not until recently. She was like his best friend and they pretty much did everything a couple would do in front of each other, within reason. He went back to reading the article and noticed it quoted a few local programmers.

Randy Fickler, one of the programmers he knew from RegTech, was upset about how much work was going offshore. This was odd because Joshua had always thought of Randy as being a cool and collected kind of guy, not prone to discussing his opinions about anything unless directly asked by someone. The other programmer was unnamed and spouted the same line as Randy.

Dancia came back wearing a black, long sleeve sweater. She found some blue jeans on the floor and slipped into them on her bed. Then she went back into the bathroom to blow dry her hair.

When she came out of the bathroom again her face was softer and her hair fuller. She sat on the bed facing the computer desk and pulled on some black boots.

"So, you driving?"

CHAPTER 7

DANCIA'S DARK GREEN Karman Ghia coupe pulled onto Broadway and cruised south towards Federal Way. The sun had slipped low on the horizon and the city was coming alive on a Saturday night. The Boise foothills were turning deep purple, the brown scrub brush and snowcaps reflected the last rays of sunlight.

She loved her car and it showed. The simple dashboard was restored to its original condition. A flower holder attached to the passenger side was purple and cream colored with a *papier-mâché* flower in it. The carpet was new and cream colored. The AM radio was original equipment and was turned down low on the local college radio station that played smooth jazz from the same era as the car.

Joshua took out the envelope he had written Glenn's address on and read it again. It was up near the Columbia Village subdivision that was built by the legendary potato king of Idaho - J. R. Simplot. The area had been enjoying a growth boom, though not to the extent of the west side of town. They turned on Federal Way and cruised east along the bench overlooking the Boise River Valley. As they came to a light a yellow Chevy Nova pulled up along side them and revved its small block engine. Dancia looked over at the young male driver. He winked at her. She looked over at Joshua and grinned. He rolled his brown eyes and grabbed the inside of the KG as she pushed down on the gas. The air breathing German engine came alive like the rolling thunder of an approaching summer storm.

Dancia's older brother was a Volkswagen mechanic and she used to help him rebuild cars from the frame up. She was a gear head long before embracing her geek side. Her Karman Ghia did not have a stock VW engine. She and her brother had mated a Porsche 914 engine to the Italian designed German car. Dancia loved to race it whenever she could against unsuspecting guys in American hot rods. Tonight the conditions were right for a little old fashioned street sweeping.

The light changed and the Nova leaped forward like a hulking metal giant, its mag wheels burning up the pavement. Dancia zipped through gears and floored the metal gas petal. Before they made it past the Maverick station the Nova had fallen behind and could not catch up to the little green Ghia with the Porsche heart. Dancia laughed as she saw the Nova receding behind in her rear view mirror. Joshua just shook his head and held on as she throttled back down to the legal speed limit. At the light to turn off Federal Way, the Nova caught up to them.

"What the hell do you have in that KG?" the Nova's driver asked from his rolled down window.

"Enough German horsepower to spank your butt, punk!" Dancia replied.

Joshua figured they were in for a fight but the Nova driver just waved at her and laughed. She pulled away from him again and he let her go this time.

They eased onto Glenn's street and slowed down, counting house numbers as they cruised. It was completely dark and they had to rely on the brilliance of streetlights and house lights. They eventually found it and both of them stared hard as they passed. It was outside of the subdivision and as such not affected by the strict covenants. The house was old and not well maintained. Tall weeds and grass that had not been mowed most of the summer mixed with all kinds of junk around the house. It was the kind of house parents forbid their kids to approach on Halloween and the same house their kids made up ghost stories about.

Dancia and Joshua exchanged looks before she sped up and went around the neighborhood. "I don't want to break into Boo Radely's house," Dancia said.

"Me neither. I wonder if he left any doors open or a key under the door mat."

"I'll make another pass." Joshua nodded his consent to that, looking around and trying to think of an easy way in.

Dancia went down the street until she found a court to turn around in. The neighborhood was quiet, a few dogs barked and you could see into homes that were lit up. People were watching TV. It was very familiar to Joshua. This was the kind of middle class neighborhood he grew up in just in a different side of town. His father worked at a technology firm and his mother was a stay at home wife until he was able to fend for himself after school and then she went back to work as a legal assistant. They had plenty of money but he never thought of his family as being rich. Most people he knew lived in his neighborhood and they all had five bedroom cookie cutter houses with two and a half car garages and a cleaning service that came every week.

Dancia was not as fortunate growing up. Her mother left them when she was five and her brother was ten. Her blue-collar father raised the kids until he was injured in a construction accident and had to retire on disability. They lived in a trailer home in an area of town long since paved over with a shopping center. Her brother Scott put himself through an automotive trade school and got a job as a mechanic at a foreign car dealership. Dancia worked odd jobs growing up just so the family could eat better. She never made enough busing tables or scooping ice-cream to set aside for her own education but she was able to contribute to her brother's schooling. In return, he taught her everything he learned at school so that she could at least be a mechanic.

She decided the best thing for her was to get an education through the military and get away from her then depressed and alcoholic father. She joined the Marines just in time to be a part of the invasion of Iraq. Her MOS was large vehicle mechanic and she was able to turn a wrench with the best of the guys, due in no small part to the training she got from her older brother. She stayed in the Marines for one enlistment and several tours in Iraq before getting out and using her GI bill to put herself through college. She met Joshua while attending Boise State and working part time at the local memory chip factory. Joshua had been out of school for almost two years now and she was still taking classes part time and working. Another semester of upper level courses and she would be able to graduate.

When they came back past Glenn's house there was a late model Ford sedan parked in the driveway and the house lights were on. Dancia pulled over in front of the house and stopped.

"What do you think, shall we pretend we're his friends or something? See if we get invited in," Joshua asked.

"Yeah, we're going out to a LAN party with Glenn and we didn't know about what happened."

"He also has some discs that he borrowed from us and we'd like to get them back. That might get us into his computer room," Joshua said.

"Ok, let's go," Dancia said opening her door and getting out.

They walked up the driveway in silence. Dancia pushed the doorbell. After what seemed like an eternity but was in actuality only a few seconds someone came to the door. It was an older woman with graying hair and a homely face. She was dressed in simple off the rack clothes and had worry lines on her pale face.

"Can I help you kids?"

Dancia spoke before Joshua could react. "Hi is Glenn around?"

The woman's face reflected shock as if she thought everyone

already knew what had happened. "Good heavens no, child. He died just yesterday."

Dancia and Joshua did their best to look shocked by the news. "We're sorry to hear that," Dancia finally said.

"We had a game with him tonight. He was going to bring us some disks with a program he was working on," Joshua said.

The woman looked back into the house for a moment and then opened the door for them to come in.

"I'm his aunt Doris from Nampa. His family asked me to look over his home until they could make arrangements to get back from Europe. They live in Norway, don't you know."

They stepped inside tentatively and looked around. It was a typical bachelor's pad, cheap furniture and sparse decorations. There was a dilapidated couch along the wall and an old TV near the front windows. A very old chrome faced VCR and a stereo that still had a turntable and eight-track player built into it. Glenn was in his late forties and Joshua got the impression he was fond of the technology that he grew up with. There was an old wooden crate with actual vinyl record albums in it, bands like ELO and Yes were visible, along with a few Journey albums. There was even a Bee-Gee's cassette in the eight-track player.

A stale musty smell snuck up on Joshua's nostrils, alerting him to the fact that very little attention was paid to cleaning the house. It smelled like a home that someone had lived in for months without actually opening a window. There was also the unmistakable stench of cat urine that hit his nose about the same time as a big old barnyard cat rubbed against his leg. Dancia let out a sneeze that caused Doris to flinch. It was followed by several more sneezes and watery eyes. She apologized politely for her allergies. Doris motioned for them to come in with a look of amusement on her face.

"Can I get you kids something to drink?" she offered.

"Yes, please, water would be great," Joshua, said trying to buy them some time in Glenn's room.

"No thank-you," Dancia said, she looked around like she was missing something and sure enough, Doris picked up on it.

"His computer is in the den, if you two would like to look around for your disks. It's just down the hall on the right."

Dancia led the way down the hall and turned into the darkened den. Joshua flipped on the light behind her and immediately felt he was in Glenn's cubicle. It was just as sparsely decorated. The walls were white and barren and there were no personalized items on his manufactured desk. A wall of cheap bookcases filled with programming and science fiction books attracted Dancia's attention. She was always curious to see what other programmers were reading. He had a smattering of O'Reilly and Microsoft Press books and quite a few hardback books by Asimov and Heinlein.

Joshua focused on the computer at the desk finding a USB plug on the front and ramming his thumb drive into it he quickly turned on the machine and waited patiently for it to boot. It automatically logged Glenn on and as soon as he was able to pull up the file manager he started transferring files to the thumb drive. Doris came in with a glass of water for Joshua. "Did you find what you were looking for?"

"Thanks, we're still looking," he said, taking the water.

"Glenn was sure into computers, we never saw him much except for the big holidays."

She looked around at the stack of old pizza boxes and the tower of soda cans stacked along the far wall. "I thought it best if I came by and cleaned up a bit before his parents came. I didn't quite know what I was getting myself into. I'll have to come back tomorrow and work most of the day to get this house presentable."

"I can't believe he's gone. How did he die?" Joshua asked his eye on the flashing blue light on the thumb drive.

"The police said he suffered a heart attack and died at his desk at work. What a terrible way to go and he was so young, so very young."

Joshua wanted to come clean with the poor woman and tell her he was the one who found Glenn but there was little comfort in telling her that. She excused herself and went back down the hall to finish cleaning in the kitchen.

Dancia came to his side and spoke softly. "You okay?"

Joshua managed a weak smile. "Yeah. Find anything useful?" She shook her head and mimicked Doris. "He was really *into* computers."

Joshua laughed and Dancia smiled. He finished the transfer and pulled the thumb drive out and shut the PC down. Dancia picked up some CD-ROMs and they left the den. Doris was filling the sink with hot water so she could mop the kitchen floor. The room smelled like ammonia cleaner.

"Thanks for letting us find the discs, Doris." Joshua said holding up the CD-ROMs.

"Oh that's no problem, you kids just let yourselves out," she said waving at them.

They left the house and got back into Dancia's Ghia. "Did you get the image?" she asked.

Joshua held up the tiny silver thumb drive and smiled.

CHAPTER 8

THE USB THUMB drive slid into his MacBook. He opened the file manager and in seconds he had all the channels and all the logs from Glenn's PC. He sat down on the floor in Dancia's room with his back to the foot of her bed.

"It worked, I have his logs and settings," Joshua said.

"Cool."

She was busy pouring over the IRC logs from Glenn's work PC. They were simple text files and she skimmed them in her editor, looking for contacts. It was very boring work so she switched on iTunes and dialed up an Internet Jazz station. A Charles Mingus saxophone solo came screeching out from her speakers. She brushed back a loose strand of her black hair and bobbed her head to the hip tune. She got turned on to Jazz from her blue-collar father. He used to play in his high-school jazz band and he was always playing old Charlie Parker or Miles Davis records when she was growing up. One time he took her and her brother to a club downtown and they heard a live four piece jazz band play. Her brother was bored and complained the whole night about having to go, but Dancia was transfixed by the energy and the freedom the musicians expressed.

Ever since that night, she refused to listen to the sugary pop music that everyone her age gushed over. It was just another thing to set her apart from everyone and everything that was popular.

Joshua transferred all the files to his desktop. He could access them faster locally and run some parsing scripts he had for searching text files. He was glad they did not have to do much to Glenn's PC, he didn't want to mess it up for a possible criminal investigation.

I'm starting to think like a detective. The thought amused him, but he had to admit that it was how he had started to view things. Not so much like a crafty gumshoe from a pulp detective novel, but more like as a program that was riddled with annoying bugs and would not compile correctly. It took patience and a clever eye for detail to properly debug a program and that just happened to be one of his strong points as a programmer.

He could track down a memory leak or a find a bad reference in code faster than most people could write such troublesome code. He could see the path of execution that the code followed as he read it. He was like a writer who could keep multiple plot threads alive in his head and still manage to write a coherent novel. This ability to juggle multiple paths of logic in his head at the same time was the hallmark of a good programmer. It also demanded total concentration the likes of which most professions did not offer on a daily basis. The ability to focus on many levels of a program at the same time required an almost Zen-like ability to clear one's mind of extraneous thought and meditate only on the task at hand.

It was tedious, demanding work that tired out a person just as much as menial labor - without the aching muscles. His brain needed a rest at the end of a long day of coding and sometimes, sitting in front of his big screen TV watching mindless entertainment was how he relaxed and other times, he just laid down and took a nap. He always wondered why his father came home after work and took a short nap before supper. Now he knew that the mental gymnastics of programming often required the brain to reset itself with a little down time.

Joshua logged into Glenn's IRC channels that he regularly

hung out in. They were very similar to the ones he had on his work PC. There was #sharp a C Sharp language channel, #coders a general programming channel and #winhack presumably for people who hacked into Windows boxes. Then there was a third channel that popped up, #0wn3d that Joshua had not seen before. He wrote down the server name for it on his scrap envelope. An idea formed in his mind.

Dancia had lit some candles. Her legs kicked up on the desk provided a surface for her keyboard

"I have an idea. I need you to log into this IRC channel and act like a curious newbie."

She took the scrap of envelope and started to dial the address into her X-Chat Aqua program. "Can I be myself or someone else?"

"You're a guy, in his early twenties, living with your parents and hacking on your Mac. I will be in there too, but I won't say anything. Don't log in for a few minutes, let me get in and just hang for a while. Then you can come in and ask a lame question."

She looked over the black rims of her glasses at him.

"Like a Japanese master, putting the student first to distract the enemy?"

Joshua nodded.

"I'll be on my lappy, and we'll talk in person. Sometimes I'll make a comment and you can react to it. But mostly I will be listening and feeding you questions," he said, as he opened his laptop and started a virtual machine with Ubuntu. "I'm going to be on Linux." Ubuntu was a popular version of Linux and Joshua ran it on all his non-Mac computers.

A virtual machine was a program that could launch an operating system inside a container where it would think it was the only operating system around. You could access the Internet, and all your real world machine hardware, all while the main operating system lurked in the background. While she waited for him to boot up a Linux virtual machine, she sat up and returned her keyboard to her desk.

"You had better go through another router, so we don't look like we are in the same place. There's a wireless access point in the apartment next door, its wide open. I use it when I want to be anonymous."

"Have you cracked it?"

She shook her head. "I'm not that kind of girl."

He was soon online, surfing like a skate boarder hitching a ride on a car bumper. "I'm in as - bitbaker. Give me few minutes to loiter and see what's going on."

She got up and moved to where he was sitting on the floor by the bed. She pulled a tennis shoe out from under the pile of clothes that they were sitting on to get comfortable. This close to him she could smell a faint hint of his cologne, it was familiar and comforting. She rubbed her arms and sat with her feet pulled up and her chin on her knees.

There were about a half dozen people in the #0wn3d chat room with names like; losing, mostaban, bet-n-man, flynn, muse, slackjawd and shemp. There was one person designated as the moderator - phong. These were all "Hacker handles", names that they used instead of their real names. You could sometimes look at their connection data and find out if they listed their real names, but most did not. Joshua was skeptical about these guys as they used what was called leet speak for their channel name. Leet or l33t was cracker slang for elite. Psycho had told him on many occasions that real Hackers didn't use leet speak much anymore, except to ridicule crackers, gamers and hacker wannabes. The method of using numbers to replace text was originally used to speed up communication on modem connections to Bulletin Board Systems and later to thwart the use of regular expressions to search text in logs. Gamers now mostly used it to trash talk to each other.

What he did find interesting was the absence of leet speak

in the aliases in use in the channel. That meant that they had already gotten over any fascination with talking in numbers and were perhaps thinking about other things besides computers. The people who hung out in the really good chat rooms could talk about more than just computer related topics. Sometimes the topics ranged from computer languages and politics to astronomy and back again.

As they watched the text scroll in the terminal window, Joshua noticed how clean and fresh Dancia's hair smelled. She was not wearing any perfume so nothing had to compete with the fragrant candles in the room. He appreciated her lack of pretense when she was with him. It was like they never had to impress each other in that way. He didn't have too many female friends and none of them were this way around him. He found it familiar and relaxing.

He didn't think she was anything less than gorgeous, he just didn't feel any sexual tension between them. She had her hair pulled back in a ponytail; it left her white neckline to contrast with the black velvet sweater she was wearing. She glanced at him and they locked eyes for a moment. Her smile was coy and innocent, but she looked away to break contact. His gaze returned to the screen where he noticed the conversation changing from the obtuse refinements of the Perl programming language to the latest Jet Li movie.

Flynn and Slackjawd were discussing who was the best the best martial arts expert in films. Mostaban interrupted with a rant about Chuck Norris being able to kick everyone's butt and the conversation halted. Eventually, Mostaban bowed out and the channel went quiet for a while.

"Ok, now's a good time to log on, nobody is chatting and they just shunned that Mostaban into submission with their silence."

Dancia got up and sat in her chair with her back perfectly straight like a diagram in an ergonomics book. Her ponytail dangled as she typed. Joshua watched her for a moment and then returned his attentions to the terminal. Her user name - Nooblet, came on with a terse announcement.

<nooblet>   Anyone here know how to cast in C++?

There was a few seconds of silence, as if the participants could not decide if she were for real.

<flynn>   Use a ten pound line and toss the whole lot into the lake. Then jump in after it.

<nooblet>   Funny. You guys real l33t in here?

<losing>   no

<nooblet>   oic

She turned and winked flirtatiously with Joshua, who smiled back at her. She was sounding like a complete loser, but looking real cute doing it. Something about a girl wearing dark rim, nerdy glasses and typing on IRC, pretending to be a guy, was more attractive than it sounded.

<phong>   *nooblet Nobody uses C++ in this room.   Try another channel.

<nooblet>   What do you guys use then?

<losing>   The Force.

<nooblet>   Right. Seriously.

<flynn>   Perl, C and some of us use Ruby.

<phong>   C.

<losing>   My vastly superior intellect can not be restricted to any one language.

<nooblet>   * nooblet laughs snidely

<nooblet>   I'm laughing at your "Superior Intellect".

<losing>   Khaaaaaaaan!

"I think you're in, Kirk," Joshua said. Dancia was not so easily convinced. "Everyone knows Star Trek lines."

<losing>   nooblet, what are you coding?

<nooblet>   Nothing, just trying to learn a new language.   I do that every couple of years, keeps the cobwebs out of the brain.   I mostly use C, some

	Perl.
<muse>	There is but one language - Perl.
<losing>	Muse knows how to do _anything_ in Perl, about ten different ways.
<losing>	*losing bows before the feet of muse.
<phong>	Perl sucks.
<nooblet>	I sleep with the Llama book under my pillow.
<muse>	You should try reading it, books make lousy head rests.
<nooblet>	I've read it so much, its pages are soft and more dog eared than a schnauzer.
<muse>	Nice.

"Perl mongers are easy to win over, as long as they think you love the language as much as they do," she said, glancing back to Joshua over the rim of her glasses.

"Agreed, keep it up. He's the ring leader of this group, I'm betting."

She started typing while she was still looking at him.

"I like Losing better."

<nooblet>	muse, do any CGI hacking in Perl?
<muse>	I've been coding Perl since before you were born, kid.
<nooblet>	Shit, I'm barely out of high school, old timer.
<losing>	That's before my time too. Muse used to use Patch, back when the dinosaurs roamed the earth.
<muse>	No, but you can believe that if you wish.
<nooblet>	WTF is Patch?
<muse>	look it up, nooblet.

"Damn, I knew he'd say that," Dancia said. Joshua shrugged; he didn't know Perl that well.

<nooblet>	*nooblet google's Patch Larry Wall

Dancia opened her browser and did the search. She found out in short order that Patch was a program Larry Wall, the creator of Perl, wrote to retrofit old source code with the latest changes to it. Some prominent hackers considered it the beginning of the open source culture. Despite the fact that few people knew about it anymore.

<nooblet>   Larry Wall is a god.

<losing>   Amen, broth-ar.

They chatted about Perl, Politics and to a lesser extent, women. Dancia made a surprisingly convincing sex-starved teenage boy. The hours whiled away, with some pauses here and there.

Dancia was getting tired of sitting. She stood up and stretched. "Let's go for a walk and get some caffeine, I've got the munchies."

CHAPTER 9

DETECTIVE PLAIT SET down his coffee and tried to focus on his computer screen. The ballistics report had come back for Henry Levine. It was most likely a consumer round. Plait figured if you had to go, you might as well have your whole head blown out. It was quick and painless but definitely not clean.

The way he was killed said a lot about the character of his killer. The killer was someone who didn't have much regard for human life and didn't care about how big a mess he left. His profile for the killer was largely incomplete. Plait had his hunch, but sometimes you had to put hunches aside and stick to the facts. If he had to guess whom the killer was this early in the game, he would have guessed it was some kind of a gang related hit. Gang members usually liked the feeling of empowerment over their intended victims. A close range, brutal death was what they preferred. However, given the age of the victim and the location of the murder, it was hard to believe that it was a gang related killing.

"Hey Bill, did you want to see me?"

It was Eric Green from the communications department. He was a middle-aged man with a friendly face and a belly that entered the room before the rest of him.

"Aren't you a Ham, Eric?"

"Sure am, W7JWIK."

Plait handed him the notebook with the radio frequency

numbers in it.

"Are you familiar with those frequencies?"

"Sure, these are local two meter repeaters here in the Treasure Valley," Eric said, handing the notebook back to Plait.

"Do you monitor any of them?"

"I have a rig in my car and one at the house out in my radio shack. So I only listen when I'm in the car or at home. We have some Ham gear at the Communications Center but it's only used in emergencies."

Plait picked up a picture of Henry Levine taken from his home. "Did you know this man?"

Eric looked at him closely before answering.

"Nope, what's his call sign?"

Plait flipped through his legal pad of notes he took at the crime scene until he found the call sign. "N7CDGR."

"No, doesn't sound familiar. But there are thousands of Hams in this area. If he was on the local repeaters, it's a good bet that we could find someone who knows him."

Plait sat back in his chair and took a sip of his coffee. The problem was, he needed to know if anyone was listening on the day Levine was killed. Something told him that it was going to be hard to find such a person. "Don't Hams have to give their call signs whenever they talk on the radio?"

"Yup, you should ID yourself before and after conversations and every ten minutes during your talk."

"Do you think we could find someone who might have been listening to this frequency on a certain day? This man was murdered and I think the killer spoke to him on the radio about a cell phone jammer he was selling on the day of the crime."

Eric put his hand to his scruffy beard and rubbed it.

"You ever meet old Joe Peterson?"

Plait shook his head; the name didn't register.

"He was a beat cop for twenty years. Before that he was a Marine. He retired, oh, about ten years ago now. Anyway,

Joe's a Ham, in fact he's one of the guys who listen to the local repeaters and makes sure people are giving their call signs and not abusing the air waves."

"Still policing eh?"

Eric smiled. "Yeah, Joe's the best. Nicest man you'll ever meet. You should give him a call or stop by his home."

"Send me his address; I think I will pay him a visit."

```
/*-------------------------------------------------*/
```

It wasn't until late in the afternoon that detective Plait managed to get out to Joe Peterson's place. The principal had called from his son's grade school to inform him that his son was in trouble for disrupting class again. He hated having to field those calls because he just knew the principal found it ironic that the police detective had a son who was constantly in his office.

Little Jimmy was not a bad kid; he was just having a hard time adjusting to being in a real school. He was in a Montessori school for three years and the class room was not as structured as a regular school so Jimmy was used to being able to wander about and work on whatever project he wanted to. Now that he was in a classroom with desks and a single teacher, he was getting less attention and having to sit for greater periods of time. It was only the first semester so he was confidant that his son would buck up and get with the program, but in the meantime his old man was going to die of embarrassment.

Joe Peterson's house was in an older neighborhood off of Cole Road. His home was old but in perfect shape and the grounds looked like they were professionally groomed.

There was a flagpole off center in the front yard with a red Marine Corps flag flying proudly under the Stars and Stripes. As Plait walked up the sidewalk to the front door, he heard a dog barking from inside.

Joe answered the door with an excited bulldog in his thick arms.

"Sorry about the noise, he's my intruder alarm."

"No problem sir. I'm detective Bill Plait from the Boise PD."

Joe looked at him with a warm smile.

"Yes, Eric mentioned you would be stopping by. Come on in Detective." Joe opened the screen door and put a big hand over the bulldog's mouth to quiet him down.

"Be quiet Sarge, he's a friend." Joe said to the dog.

Plait stepped inside and waited for Joe to shut the door and put the dog down. Sarge came over and started sniffing Plait's shoes, it was apparent from the animal's playful demeanor that he was not a vicious killer. Plait reached down and rubbed the squat dog behind his white ears. Sarge let out a muffled bark and then was quite content.

"He likes you Detective. Usually he's slow to warm up to strangers."

"I've always been a dog person."

Plait stood up and shook Joe's out stretched hand. "You can call me Bill."

"Bill, can I get you something to drink?"

"No thanks, I'm fine. Did Eric say what I was interested in?"

Joe motioned for them to sit down in the front living room. Plait took a seat on the couch and Sarge followed him for more affections. Joe sat down on his favorite reading chair, surrounded by bookshelves stocked with military history and electronics books.

"He said you were investigating the death of Henry Levine."

"Murder actually. He was shot in the head execution style."

Joe shook his head in disgust. "Man what is the world coming to? Henry was a harmless old man never mean to anyone. A lot of Hams are going to miss him."

Plate looked around the small room. It was evident that Joe lived by himself, there was nothing womanly about the decor of his living room. From the dark patterns of the furniture fabrics to the framed pictures of Marines in combat and military vehicles, Joe was interested in the kinds of things that only men truly appreciated. Plait felt right at home in the place and he wished that he could spend some time chatting with Joe about his career in the Marines and his time on the force, but today he had a job to do.

"Did you know Henry at all?"

Joe nodded, his crystal blue eyes shined from under bushy white eyebrows. "He came to our club meetings quite regularly and he also checked into the morning net we run on the local repeater. I didn't tune in every morning for the net, but when I did, he always seemed to have something interesting to say. If memory servers, he used to work on the rail lines, years ago," Joe said.

"Did he ever mention anything about selling his gear online?"

Joe thought about that for a moment then shook his head slowly. "You know, I've tried to recall anything about the man that would have seemed strange or out of place in the last few days and I keep coming up blank."

"Did you happen to hear him on the radio yesterday at all?"

"No. But there is more than one repeater here in town; he may have been on another one. I try and listen to both when I can, but yesterday I had some other things going on and was in and out most of the day. Tell you what I *can* do though, I can contact some of my other Ham buddies and see if anyone heard him talking."

"That would be great, Joe," he said taking out a business card from his jacket pocket. "Can you give me a call if you find out anything?"

"You betcha I will. Do you have any leads on the case at all?"

Plait shook his head slowly. "Looks like a random murder,

except for the manner in which he was killed. Mr. Levine was a fairly honest man, near as I can tell. Going to be hard to pin this on drugs, it could be a revenge killing. But we haven't found anyone who had a grudge with him."

"I wish I still had a badge, I'd love to help you out on this one. I'd hate to see something like this go unsolved."

Plait agreed. He stood up and shook Joe's hand. "Good to meet you Joe, I wish it were under better circumstances."

"Likewise Bill, likewise, I'll get right on the phone and I should have an answer for you soon on whether anyone heard Henry on the radio yesterday."

"Thanks, oh and if you would keep this off the air waves, our killer might still be listening."

"Will do, sir."

He let the detective out the front door and held back a panting Sarge. "Have a great and wonderful day Bill!"

Bill waved goodbye as he headed back to his car. Something told him Joe wouldn't find out anything, but it was a nice way to end his day, making a new acquaintance. Joe probably appreciated having something to investigate.

CHAPTER 10

DANCIA LIVED ON 4th street, about a block away from the Flying M Espresso Coffee House. They put on their heavy coats and walked down the street to the popular hang out spot. The night air was crisp. Joshua brought along his lap top so they could continue monitoring the chat room using the coffee shop's free Wi-Fi.

The Flying M was a favorite local hang out for art lovers and creative types. The brown brick building contained big comfy furniture and some of the best coffee in Boise served by a friendly staff that loved the place as much as the many varied customers. Dancia hung out there all the time, catching up with her friends from school and consuming fresh baked goods and gallons of delicious coffee.

Even on a cold, November night, there were people sitting outside on the wooden benches absorbed in conversations and sipping coffee. The smell of zesty Italian sauce lingered from the pizza shop at the other end of the building. Dancia spotted someone she knew outside but just waved at her briefly as they headed inside to warm up.

Inside there was a modest crowd for a Saturday night. Joshua grabbed a seat on the black leather couch and Dancia went to stand in line to get their coffee. She immediately started chatting with other people in line. Joshua opened up his computer and signed back into the IRC channel. It still showed nooblet and six others logged in, but nobody was chatting. They picked a good time to get away.

Joshua looked around and took in the atmosphere of the coffee house. He used to hang out there all the time when he was a student. But lately, he only found himself coming in when he wanted to get out of his apartment and still be found by his friends. When he didn't want to be found, he headed to the airport and worked on his airplane. He was always polishing the chromed metal skin or fixing some little part that was broken like a piece of fabric trim in the cabin.

Dancia came back with two big white cups of coffee and a large cookie for herself. She sat down beside him and motioned to the computer. "Anything going on?"

"No, it's dead quiet."

They sipped their coffee and watched the other people talking and laughing. Most were either students or arty types as the house had a fairly well known local art collection on display.

"There's Melina." Dancia pointed out her friend across the way, sketching patrons with a charcoal stick on a large pad of paper. As if she had heard Dancia, Melina noticed her and got up. She sat down next to Dancia.

"What's up stranger?"

"Not much, just came out for some caffeine then it's back to the ones and zeros," Dancia replied, taking the drawing pad from her friend.

"You are so talented girl."

Melina grinned sheepishly. She was a short, brunette with straight hair and big brown eyes. She was wearing a tight T-shirt with her belly exposed and faded blue jeans. It was warm in the coffee house and everyone slipped out of their heavy coats upon coming inside.

"Who's your friend?" Melina asked.

"Oh, I'm sorry. Melina, Joshua. Joshua, Melina."

Joshua waved and said hello. She nodded and replied, "Hi,

I'm Dancia's frustrated art friend."

"I'm her geek friend who keeps her at the computer all the time."

Melina raised an eyebrow. "Mmmm, sounds kinky."

Dancia hit her in the head with her drawing and gave it back to her. They started chatting about common friends and who was dating whom, Joshua quickly tuned them out as he looked around the room. There was a good mix of students reading textbooks, computer nerds staring at laptops and a few older people talking at a table.

Near the back of the room, sitting under a neon clock was an older man peering at a laptop. He had thinning brown hair and wore a faded flower shirt and tight blue jeans with well-worn cowboy boots. It was Larry Taggert the UNIX guy from Joshua's office. Joshua felt an urge to go over and say hi, but it looked like he was absorbed in reading something. Larry was not the most social person and Joshua thought it was kind of strange to see him in a public place. Of course he got that feeling about seeing most anyone he worked with outside of the work place. You work with people every day in a given environment and you start to associate them with that environment. When you see them outside of that environment, your brain has to reconcile that and sometimes it just doesn't seem right.

A crowd of people came inside talking loudly and drawing attention to themselves. It was Tripp and his nerdy film friends. There were three of them and they immediately came over to Joshua.

"Hey it's the geek squad," Tripp said, slapping Joshua's hand in a lazy five. "What's up?"

There was another guy named Dave who was tall and had tight, curly red hair. Joshua recognized him as having worked at the local art film theater. A girl was with them; she was kind of heavy and wore glasses. She was carrying a Variety magazine under her arm and dressed all in black. Her name was Suz and she was a film critic for the local free paper.

"Just taking a coffee break, what kind of trouble are you guys into tonight?"

Tripp fell into the couch beside Joshua. "We just saw that new indie film at the Flicks. It was pretty cool, but we thought they could have done better."

Dave nodded and Suz frowned. "Yeah, they're not going to like my review. But then nobody ever does," Suz said.

Suz was famous for never liking any film she reviewed. She was sometimes creative in her trashing but mostly she was just brutally honest.

"Speaking of film reviews, how's the site coming?" Tripp asked.

"It's coming. Dancia finished the data model and now I just have to tidy up the view, tweak the style sheet a bit. You guys want to bash on it for a while?"

Tripp shook his head. "Not tonight, we're going to grab some brews and head over to Suz's place to watch *Brazil*."

Brazil was a heady take on Orwell's *1984* and a really long film. It was one of Tripp's all time favorites and the kind of film that the more you watched it, the more you found things that you missed before. Joshua actually didn't mind watching it, because it had some weird computers in it and it was just plain bizarre.

"You and DC want to join us?"

Joshua was startled by the offer but politely refused. Tripp hit him on the shoulder in the way that guys do when they think their friend is about to score. Joshua shot him a look that said, "Get lost!" and Tripp stood up. Dancia and Melina were still chatting about stuff and didn't really pay them much attention.

"Ok, we're out of here, see you kids later," Tripp said as they headed back out into the cold, already arguing about the lighting in the film they had just seen.

After they left, Joshua looked back down at the laptop. There was some idle chatting going on about the latest Intel processors.

He tapped Dancia on her knee and she turned to him.

"I think we need to be getting back," he said, pointing to the screen.

She glanced at it a moment and then returned to Melina. "It was good to see you again girl."

"Yeah, same here. You guys going anywhere interesting?"

Dancia smiled. "We have a project going on back at my place, we could be coding for a while."

"I just don't understand your fascination with computers. I find them cold and boring."

"Not everyone can be a talented, starving artist."

Melina shrugged. "That would be pretty boring. I guess I'll draw some more people, and see if she shows up again. Don't you hate it when you see someone you would like to get to know better and circumstances align to stop it from happening?"

Dancia nodded. "Maybe you'll get lucky and she'll come back."

"She's prolly not gay anyway, so I shouldn't get my hopes up."

That got Joshua's ear. "Whom are you guys talking about?"

"Some chick Melina saw in here last night. She's totally got the hots for her."

"What does she look like?" Joshua asked.

Melina unfolded a few pages of her sketchpad and showed Joshua a portrait she drew of the girl. She was very pretty and you could tell Melina had given some extra attention to the drawing. It captured the girl's elegant chin line and dimples. Joshua thought she was very striking, but he had not seen her before.

"If you see her again, and she's a breeder, get her number for me," he said with a smile.

Melina laughed. "Sure thing. Might as well play matchmaker at that point. But if you go out with her you have to let me follow you guys around and draw her."

"Deal."

Dancia pushed Joshua in a playful manner. "Let's get going, we got some work to do."

Joshua closed his lappy and put his coat back on. The girls hugged and then Dancia stood up and put her coat on and zipped it up. "See you around."

"Bye guys, see you later."

They left the coffee house and started walking back to Dancia's apartment building.

"Don't you think Melina is cute?"

"Sure, she seemed pretty cool. Do you guys know each other from school?"

Dancia smiled. "No, we've been friends forever, went to grade school together."

"Tripp and I have known each other that long too. I don't know why I still hang with him, we don't exactly have much in common anymore."

"I believe you can't always shake your best friends that easily. Even if you move to the other side of the country and lead completely different lives, you can call them up and chat knowing that they are still one of the few people that really know you."

Joshua thought about that for a moment as they walked in silence. Ever since his parents died, he had been pretty much alone in life. All of his relatives were living back East and he only got together with them every few years. Tripp was like a brother, someone you could hang with and not have to communicate verbally with all the time. They always looked out for each other and kept up with events in their lives, just like family would. He even had Joshua over to his parent's house for the holidays. Sometimes Joshua used Tripp's father as a sounding board for advice, like he used to talk to his own dad. Greg was pretty cool about it; he always made time for Joshua and would invite him over for dinner just so he and Tripp's mom could find out how he was doing.

"As Tripp is so fond of saying, 'No man is a failure who has friends'. I think that's from *It's A Wonderful Life*."

"I love that movie. Watch it every Christmas."

"Me too."

When they got back to Dancia's bedroom, they found the IRC group engrossed in conversation about the merits of Flash script. A new person had joined the group named Shemp. He was arguing with Losing about how Flash was more than just a way to make moving images on the web. He was not getting anywhere with the largely Perl oriented coders of the group.

Joshua motioned for Dancia to join in. "Jump in, but stay pro Perl."

She flexed her fingers and began to type.

\<nooblet\>	Flash is for Windows weenies. Nobody designs web pages with that unless they are art types.
\<losing\>	Exactly my point, nooblet. This guy thinks you can use Flash script to do complicated CGI type stuff.
\<shemp\>	All I'm saying is if you really look at the code, it's not that different than JavaScript. It has the capability to do great stuff. Just nobody has done anything with it yet, except for graphics stuff.
\<losing\>	Give me access to CGI bin and let me code with Perl. Screw that punk Flash crap.
\<nooblet\>	Amen broth-ar.

There was another long pause where nobody typed anything. Joshua was reading through some chats that Glenn had had with Shemp about Flash. Glenn was more in line with Shemp on the topic. He came across a conversation they had one night about hypnotists. Shemp was convinced that he could write a Flash script that would hypnotize a person. Glenn was skeptical about it and offered links to sites that disproved the idea. But Shemp was unconvinced.

"Mention that you saw a magician hypnotize someone once. I want to see what Shemp says to that. He got into the topic with Glenn once here in the logs."

Dancia thought about it for a second before typing.

\<nooblet\>	I saw this magic show yesterday where the guy actually hypnotized this lady and made her think she was a monkey.
\<losing\>	Did she fling some shit?
\<nooblet\>	No. But she did act very simian-like. It was such a load of crap.
\<shemp\>	Hypnotizing is legitimate, maybe it was real.
\<nooblet\>	This guy was a charlatan and the girl was obviously in on it.
\<losing\>	What the hell were you doing at a magic show?

Dancia shrugged and looked at Joshua for her reply.

"Tell him you had to take your little sister," he said.

\<nooblet\>	I had to take my little sister to it for her birthday. They even had clowns. I hate clowns.
\<losing\>	Me too. Clowns creep me out.
\<shemp\>	I hypnotized someone once with a Flash script.
\<losing\>	Shut up!
\<nooblet\>	Hang it up Shemp, nobody believes in that crap.
\<shemp\>	Whatever, I know what I did and the person I did it to was completely under my control.
\<losing\>	That's how he gets women to go out with him.
\<nooblet\>	*nooblet laughs hysterically.
\<shemp\>	I could have made him do anything.

Joshua looked up.

"Shit!" he said, as he realized that Shemp could be the killer they were looking for.

Dancia turned to him. "What?"

"Do you think he could make someone kill themselves?"

Dancia stared at him for a moment, as she realized that she might be talking to the killer. "Is Shemp the one?"

"Possibly, but we don't know much about him. Let's start searching the logs for his name, maybe he will let something slip."

When Dancia looked back to the screen, she saw an odd exchange and then shemp logged off.

```
<muse>      39430
<shemp>     k
<shemp>         has quit (Read error: Connection reset by peer)
```

"What was that all about? What does that number mean?" Dancia asked.

"I don't know. I'm switching channels to #coders. See if anyone knows. Keep searching those logs from work."

She nodded and started doing regular expressions in Vi to find Shemp or that number. Joshua had finished his search and did not find anything.

In #coders, he tossed out his question. There were only five people in the channel. The odds were not too good he would come up with anything.

```
<jjones>    Anyone know what 39430 might refer too?    It's
            just a number to me.
```

To his surprise, someone came back. It was Steve, his buddy from over on the Boise Bench.

```
<w7rbyy>    Hey Joshua.
<jjones>    What's up Steve?    Any idea what that number
            might mean?
<w7rbyy>    Sounds familiar, oh yeah, that's a frequency on
            80 meters.
<jjones>    A Ham band?
<w7rbyy>    Yes, why are you asking about a Ham freq?
<jjones>    It's a long story.  You busy?
```

It was just after midnight on a Saturday night. Steve was probably working in his Ham shack.

<w7rbyy>   Nope, just testing some old tubes for the Collins
                rig.
<jjones>   Mind if I stop by?
<w7rbyy>   Nope.

Joshua closed his laptop and stood up. "Get your coat back on, we're going for a ride."

"What did you find?" Dancia asked, getting up and looking around for her coat. Her log search had yielded two similar numbers both of which she memorized. She had an uncanny ability to memorize random numbers and little bits of data that seemingly had no connection to anything. She rarely wrote to-do notes to herself either.

"It's a Ham radio frequency and we're heading over to Steve's house to see if we can hear these guys chatting."

"Steve Lancy?" Dancia asked, tentatively. She was hoping it was someone else.

Joshua nodded. "Yeah."

Dancia averted her eyes. "Ok, but you're driving."

CHAPTER 11

IT WAS A short ride down Federal Way past the Boise Depot to Steve's house. The heater in Joshua's Porsche barely had time to get warmed up. Steve's house was a three-story custom home that over looked the city and the surrounding foothills. It was built in the mid 70's and updated through the years by his parents. When they wanted to retire and move to Arizona, they sold the house to their only son.

Steve moved into the basement and rented out the main two floors. He charged outrageous rent and people paid for the spectacular views and close proximity to the down town area. He could almost live off the rent, but chose instead to keep his System Administration job at a local business.

He usually worked the graveyard shift, which left his evenings off free to talk all night on his Ham radios. The best propagation occurred at night on most High Frequency or HF bands. His position along the Boise Bench also aided in getting his signal out to the world and in bringing in signals from all over the planet. He had made contacts with other Hams in all 50 states including Hawaii and Alaska and was starting to work other countries in Asia and Europe. There was something about talking to another human being who lived far away by bouncing your signal off the upper atmosphere that was both technically cool and fashionably quaint in the modern world of instant digital communication.

In the back yard he had raised a forty foot main tower with a rotating beam for 20, 40, 60 and 80 meters, letting him point the antenna he was using in any direction by remote control. The setup was not uncommon for Hams active in HF signal chasing. He was in the process of raising a second tower that would be for 6, and 10 meters. Right now he was using a simple inverted dipole wire antenna for those bands. The backyard of his house looked like a small antenna farm, with guide wires running all over the yard. It made mowing the grass a bit tricky, but his renters didn't have to worry about that, because Steve gladly did the yard work so they didn't have to. He preferred that the renters didn't even go in the back yard. There was a large wooden deck on the main level of the house and a small deck on the top level, so they could get outside without going down to the backyard.

Joshua parked in the roundabout in the front yard, leaving the main driveway free. He and Dancia got out and walked to the side of the house down a narrow footpath to concrete steps that lead to the basement level door. Steve had turned on the porch light for them so they could see to walk down the stairs. Joshua rapped his knuckles on the door a few times and after a minute Steve opened the door to let them in.

Steve was in his late thirties and wore black-framed "geek" glasses. His hair was salt and pepper where it once had been black and was cut military short, he wore the fashionable goatee and side burns popular with younger men. He was slim and stood a few inches over six foot. His face had a ready smile as he recognized Dancia.

"Hey guys, come on in."

"Hi Steve," Dancia said, as she came inside before Joshua. She waltzed into the place like it was her own home, as she often did at Joshua's place. "Hey pug," Steve casually said as she passed.

"Hope we're not intruding," Joshua said, wondering what

that exchange was all about.

"Oh no, I never turn down visitors on a Saturday night, or is it morning now?"

Steve's basement was the ultimate nerd pad. There was a small kitchenette off to the right and a narrow home theater to the left of the entrance with a fireplace in the corner and a plasma screen tuned to a Right Wing news channel. They followed Dancia down the short hall that lead to the main room where he had all his radio and computer gear. Dancia glanced briefly across the hall where Steve's bedroom was. The door to his Ham shack had a picture of a big red circle with a line through a Microsoft Windows logo on it. Steve was somewhat fanatical about his dislike for the software giant.

Steve called the room a "shop" as it was still unfinished and had thick throw rugs on top of the concrete floor. A space heater was running near his main workbench. The room had large picture windows that looked out over the city and the surrounding foothills. It was an impressive view during the daytime, but not at night. Only their own reflections looked back at them through the windows like a mirror.

The lighting was from over head fluorescent tubes of the kind most people used in their garages. He had one old black desk with a matching wooden chair with springs that let you lean back comfortably in it. He had two twenty one inch LCD monitors on swing out metal mounts and a wireless keyboard with a trackball mounted to the right arm of the chair. His computers all ran Linux, of course, and the monitors displayed custom programs that let him monitor his radios and his servers remotely.

Behind the monitors were several custom built black wooden shelves containing high-end Japanese amateur radio gear. He had the latest and most expensive gear money could buy; the kind of radios that most Hams only dreamed about owning. He had them hooked up to antenna switch boxes and rotators. A nice cordless headset rested next to the keyboard.

His workbench was about twelve feet long and ran along the same wall facing the city. It had all manner of electronic test equipment. Everything from simple meters to advanced waveform monitors and temperature controlled soldering irons. Much of his equipment was new but a good bit of it was old and probably no longer manufactured. He loved to recondition old tube radios and he had some ancient devices that looked like they came from an old black and white science fiction movie.

Every few feet along the bench there was another unfinished radio or electronics project of some kind. Miles of coax cables and hundreds of test leads and cables with different connectors on them lined the space under the bench hanging from nails. All along the length of the bench were miss matched drawers filled with little electronic bits and pieces, tiny plastic drawers that fishermen used to keep their lures in, Steve stored - ceramic insulators, resisters, capacitors and tiny knobs.

There was an entire corner dedicated to old antennas and the parts for fabricating antennas out of metal tubes and rolls of wires from heavy gauge electrical wire to thin electronics wiring. Several antennas lay unfinished and waiting for some attention.

The middle of the room was filled with metal racks full of old radios and miscellaneous electrical devices making the room look like either a radio repair shop or a swap meet for electronics geeks. Towards the far right there was a rudimentary machine shop where Steve was known to build his own radio cases and just about anything that he dreamed up that needed a box to live in.

The back of the room seemed to be dedicated to a completely different hobby - guns. Steve was a proud member of the NRA and owned a respectable little collection of firearms. He had a bench dedicated to cleaning and working on his guns. He even had a nice Dillon Progressive reloading press in the corner.

There was an American flag pinned to the back wall, just in case anyone questioned his loyalties.

"So what can I do for you guys?" Steve asked. He was wearing jeans and a black T-shirt that had a penguin armed with a big machine gun from a video game.

"We need to listen to that frequency to see if we can hear anyone talking."

Steve moved over to his Ham station and plopped down in the chair. Its springs creaked under his weight. He moved a monitor up out of his way and fiddled with a digital radio dial.

"I've been monitoring it ever since you asked about it, nothing going on. Tuning around, I found some chatter a few clicks up the dial but they were talking French or Spanish or something."

Dancia and Joshua looked at each other and frowned. If they were referring to a Ham frequency there was no guarantee that it was somehow code for another band. They may have been intending to talk at a different time on the given frequency. There were just too many possibilities.

"Steve, do you need all this fancy gear to just listen to that band?"

"Heck no, you could listen to this on a commercial receiver with a simple wire antenna," Steve replied, still tuning around the band.

Joshua looked around the room at the stacks of old radios, "Do you think we could borrow a radio to do some listening with? It would only be for a few days, maybe a week."

Dancia started to wander around the room, her dark eyes washing over in all the details. Steve got up and headed for the racks. "Sure, I got plenty of old rigs that would work for you."

He pulled an old brown radio with a big dial on its face off the rack and hauled it over to an empty spot on the long test bench. Moving around the bench like a surgeon around an operating table, he quickly assembled the parts and pieces for a complete radio.

"You can set this up just about anywhere and it should work with a simple dipole antenna. Hang on a few and I'll make you one."

Joshua nodded as he watched Steve pull some coax cable and start building the wire antenna. Joshua never really was into radio technology, it all seemed too old fashioned and low tech to him. But he loved to watch a skilled tech build something from nothing. He often spent many hours watching shows on TV that were about people making things like motorcycles or cars. It was a part of the unwritten Hacker ethos that fueled his curiosity for things mechanical as well as things digital. When he was a kid, he lived inside those books with detailed exploded views of everything from microwave ovens to aircraft carriers. If it were manmade, Joshua was always curious about how it was put together.

Dancia was over looking at the open gun locker. She noticed a few new additions to Steve's collection. There was a nice new Ruger 10/22 with a black laminate stock sitting in a cleaning rack. She ran her fingers down the metal barrel and took in the smell of the laminate and the gun oil. It brought back very real experiences that she had tried unsuccessfully to lay to rest. She recalled the last time she and Steve were on the local outdoor range plinking with rifles. Steve loved guns and was very macho about his knowledge of them, but he was a lousy shot. He preferred making modifications and cleaning his pieces to actually putting rounds down range at a target. He didn't even like to hunt.

That was fine by her, since shooting was more than enough to trigger uncomfortable memories from her time in the sand box.

She had first met Steve a few years ago when she was hired to assist him in the UNIX shop where he worked. She was the gofer and back up tape jockey, eager to learn UNIX and system administration. He was the wise, older guru who seemed to know all the obscure inside knowledge about computer systems. She was a quick apprentice and after about six months she had learned more than he knew and had bagged him in the process. Not only was he limited in his computer skills; he was not that interesting physically for her to bother with for too long. She realized he compensated for not knowing everything he claimed about computers, by dazzling people with his knowledge about radios and electronics. Whenever anyone got too deep in the details of something that he didn't really know very well, Steve would somehow manage to steer the conversation back to radio theory, his comfort zone.

To Dancia, once she figured this out about Steve, she became less interested in him and soon broke off their relationship. She quickly got a better job and was making more than him even though her computer experience was about one quarter that of his. Guys like Steve found their little niche and then never cared to advance further, fearing the ranks of management or change in general. Steve was in charge of the UNIX group at his company and he had no ambitions to move up or move on. He was a big fish in a little pond and he liked it that way. Not two months after she had moved on, he had hired another newbie girl and was cheerfully passing on his wisdom to her.

```
/*-------------------------------------------------*/
```

Steve finished up the antenna and started going over how to tune the radio and set it up with Joshua. Joshua listened very astutely, making Dancia smile as she watched them. She knew enough about radios from working with Steve to have confidently set up the little Hallicrafters receiver by herself. But it was still cute the way Joshua soaked up new and interesting things. He was like a kid on Christmas day, waiting for his father to finish building a new toy, so he could play with it.

They were just finishing up as she came back to them. Joshua picked up the radio and Steve gathered up all the accessories.

"Looks like we're set. Steve, thanks again for your help man."

"No problem. If you have any questions, don't hesitate to call."

"Thanks Steve, it looks like we'll be busy for a few days anyway," Dancia commented as she held the door for them.

Joshua headed out the side door and up the stairs to the car, Steve and Dancia held back. He waited until Joshua was out of earshot before speaking.

"So, are you two seeing each other?" Steve said his tone smug.

"Maybe. It's really not your business, Steve."

"You're right. Does he know about us?"

"No, and please keep it that way for now, okay?" She glanced at him over the top of her black rim glasses. He laughed and headed out the door first. "No problem, Pug."

"Stop calling me that," she said, hitting him in the back. Pug was his nickname for her when they were going out together. He thought she was a little firecracker, which reminded him of a fireplug and somehow he managed to get pug out of all that. She really didn't like pet names and that one really annoyed her. It reminded her that she was short and possibly fat. He liked using it because it annoyed her. They made for a real dysfunctional couple, which had a lot to do with why they broke up.

Out at the car Joshua had tucked the radio into the back seat and covered it with a throw blanket that he kept in the trunk. Steve handed Joshua the antenna parts. "Give me a buzz if you have any troubles."

"Will do. Thanks a bunch Steve."

"No problem, just remember to tune around, you may get

lucky, providing they stay on that band. Let me know how it goes, you got my curiosity up too."

Joshua shook Steve's hand as Dancia got into the Porsche.

"We will," Joshua said, stepping into the driver's seat.

Steve watched them pull out and then went back inside.

CHAPTER 12

THE RED NUMERALS on the clock in the kitchen read one forty-five in the morning, but the apartment was neither dark nor quiet. The back of the friendly brown receiver was a warm yellow color as the tubes heated up. The two large semi-circle dials on its front panel gave the faint impression of a barnyard owl. One was for band selection and the other for fine-tuning. The interface hearkened back to simpler days and consisted of two dials flanking a signal meter, a row of knobs and several switches extended across the bottom, each with clearly readable labels. The old Hallicrafters SX-100 was a legend in its day and still pulled in signals with a clarity and warmth that no modern transistor radio could ever hope to equal.

There was no sound coming from the external speaker. Joshua was still stringing up the simple wire dipole antenna and letting the radio's tubes warm up. He taped the thin wires to the ceiling in a north-south direction, while standing on a kitchen chair. He was awake and full of enthusiasm. He had never listened to short wave radio growing up and had somehow felt like he had been deprived. He remembered his dad talking about listening to far away commercial stations when he was a kid in the sixties, but his dad didn't keep his old radio and so Joshua never had the opportunity to be exposed to it. In an age when the personal computer was your conduit to the world over the Internet, the idea of pulling in signals out of a wavering atmosphere seemed hopelessly old fashioned and low tech.

Joshua had a thing for old tech; he drove a car and flew an airplane that were both from the fifties. His clothes reflected that time period in their simplicity and classic styling. This new toy was just as exciting to him as getting a new laptop. He also loved the romance of old tech. Something about consumer items from that decade left him feeling warm inside like eating fresh baked cookies or sipping warm peppermint tea on a cold winter night. Back then things had curves and class and warmth that the mass-produced, perfectly manufactured items of the today lack. There was no denying the simplicity and elegance of an iPod, but it could not hold a candle to a 1958 Corvette or a Western Cutlery sheath knife.

/*---*/

Dancia was on his laptop browsing for news on Zemo and monitoring the IRC chat room. She was not the least bit intrigued with the radio. Having dated Steve for several months, she had heard him waxing over and listening to his radios for long enough to learn to loath them. It was not that operating radios was something that only men did; there were plenty of women Ham operators. It just seemed to her that it was a technical hobby that still required you to know something about how your equipment worked and how signal propagation worked, which tended to be a major turn off for most females. Most of what the men talked about on the air was related to the technical nature of the hobby. It just was not that interesting to her. Sometimes they talked about politics and that usually led to rants that had a decidedly Right Wing slant, which made her gag. She never could figure out why more women didn't become Hams and talk about womanly things. Even idle gossip would be more interesting than signal reports.

She let Joshua play with the radio and occasionally watched him fuss over it like it was some kind of new arrival. Mostly she just surfed and listened to some jazz on a radio station that simulcast on the web out of the San Francisco Bay area. Eventually, she turned on the big screen TV and found an old black and white movie. The cable guide said it was *Rebecca*, 1940, and stared Laurence Olivier and Joan Fontaine. After coming in near the beginning, she became engrossed in the story and soon abandoned the laptop for the easy chair. The black and white movie shined brilliantly on Joshua's big plasma TV. She snuggled under the afghan and watched the show.

/*---*/

Joshua sat down at the Hallicrafters and switched the knob from Standby to Receive. A warm, soft sputtering static filled the air from the square speaker resting beside the radio. He adjusted the band dial and then started tuning around, looking for conversations. He didn't have to go far before he found a Ham chatting away about his family ranch in Colorado. Joshua thought about the signal bouncing over the Rockies and traveling down the wires of his antenna and getting converted by the radio's tubes into something that could be understood. The magic of radio.

He sat at the kitchen table and listened to the radio for another hour before becoming tired. He caught himself dosing off several times and finally decided around two forty-five in the morning that he had better go to bed. He dragged himself away from the warm, glowing radio and into the dark living room where Dancia was watching some old black and white movie.

"I'm going to bed. I left the radio on the frequency we got from Shemp. Feel free to listen, turn it off when you are done."

/*---*/

She looked away from the picture and nodded. He looked really tired, his eyes baggy and his shoulders hunched. She didn't expect him to have lasted this late into the night. Joshua turned and padded back down the hall to his bedroom. Dancia returned her attention to the troubles of the new Mrs. De-Winter.

An hour later, the movie was over and Dancia was bored. She opened the laptop and checked into the chat rooms she was monitoring. There was little activity so she went into her favorite Linux chat room where there were hundreds of users on and plenty of activity. She started to get the munchies and went into the kitchen to see what Joshua had to snack on. His refrigerator was nearly empty, so she poked around in the cupboards for some crackers or chips or maybe some cookies. She found a box of Ritz crackers that had an unopened sleeve in it. She took out the sleeve and put the box back. He had a wine rack on the counter and she really wanted to open a bottle.

Joshua's taste in wine tended to lean toward local Idaho red wines. Red wine gave her a headache, she pulled out a light colored chardonnay from the Sawtooth Winery and decided that would do. She opened the drawer where she remembered his wine opener was and opened the bottle. She let it breathe while she searched for a wine glass. She found some in a top cabinet that she was too short to reach. Dragging a kitchen chair over, she grabbed a glass and set it beside the wine. Scooting the chair back, she noticed the orange glow of the radio on the table. It was casting interesting shadows on the dark kitchen walls from the fine mesh grill on the back of the radio.

She decided to sit down with her crackers and wine and give the radio a listen. She turned up the volume and turned the tuner knob slowly across the band. There was a signal that was weak and then as she turned the knob slowly, it came in stronger. It sounded like a large man's voice and he was talking in French. Dancia took French in high school and her first two years in college. She was pretty good at it but she didn't use her skill very often and was not very fluent. She did manage to follow along to what the man was talking about.

It was poetry. She caught references to Shakespeare and several modern American poets. Dancia wondered if the man was in France or Canada as she listened to the one sided conversation. Hams tended to ramble on for long periods of time on the HF bands before signing over to the other party. This was mostly do to the conditions but was also just a tradition. There was no timing out or other interruptions and it let the other party take a break and gather their thoughts for a rebuttal.

When it was finally time for the other Ham to talk, it was another man, younger and more hip in his phrasing. Dancia listened and became enthralled with the conversation. They were discussing poetry and reciting favorite passages back to each other. She wondered briefly if they were gay but she didn't get that impression from their tone and inflection. They were just two fans of the medium talking about what they enjoyed most about their favorite poets. Dancia liked poetry, but she had not read much in quite some time. In high school she went through her Emily Dickinson phase and then moved on to the British poets and finally wound up appreciating Bob Dylan.

They started talking about a poem called "Howl" by Allen Ginsberg - a Beat Generation poet and friend of Jack Kerouac and William S. Burroughs. Dancia had read Kerouac's *On the Road* back when she first heard the song "Hey, Jack Kerouac", by the alternative band *10,000 Maniacs*. It launched her on a cross-country trip to pick up the Karman Ghia with Melina, before Dancia went into the Marines. It was the best time she ever had and it was her last rudderless voyage before her life took a purposeful turn. The military matured her in ways that civilian life could not and going to college helped her make sense of the madness of war and the questions she had about her station in life.

She found the poem on line and started to read it as she listened to them talking about it. It was an epic poem, banned at one point for obscenity and admired by nearly everyone. She

liked it immediately and wanted to talk about it, but could only
listen to the two poetry fans on the brown receiver. The older
Ham seemed to have lived during the fifties and had been turned
on to the Beat Generation first hand. He was well versed in
Jazz and Beatnik culture. The younger man was less impressed
with the work and tried to insist that his generation had its own
crazy time making sense of life. He quoted modern poets and
writers like Neal Stephenson, Eliot Katz and Levi Asher. He
mused on how the Internet has shaped his generation more than
any other medium has changed a generation. The older man
seemed to scoff at that notion, but he had to concede that the
Internet revolution was only just beginning and that history will
only record those alive at its birth that caused it to come into
existence. Those early pioneers of the medium may be lost to the
winds of time when they are quickly replaced by the generation
that perfects the idioms used in the global voice.

Dancia found the conversation intellectually stimulating,
like a good college lecture on philosophy. Just when she was
beginning to enjoy herself the conversation ended and the
foreign voices signed off with their call signs. She typed them
down in her editor and saved them to the desktop. She would be
listening for them again, regardless of whether they ever heard
this Shemp guy talking again or not. She tuned around the band
for a while, and then grew bored with the radio. She left it on the
channel that Joshua was listening to and turned down the gain so
she could surf and read some more poets of her generation.

She checked the IRC chat room and found it dead quiet.
Shemp was in the chat room and so were a few others, but
nobody had been talking.

<nooblet>   Who speaks for our generation?

There was no reply. She had hoped that Shemp was around.
It was nearly four in the morning; most people in North America
were long in bed. She picked up her glass of wine and finished
it in one drink. Maybe it was time to turn in. She checked the

temperature on the weather widget. It was twenty-two degrees Fahrenheit. "Colder than flijigans," she said out loud. She was wearing a sweater but it was not a tight weave and her arms were feeling chilled as she rubbed them with both hands.

She remembered a particularly cold night in the desert after seeing action along the road to Baghdad. She was in a ditch off the side of a road in the middle of nowhere with four other squad mates. Their HUMVEE was disabled and they were waiting for help from the convoy. That was the longest, coldest night of her life. The temperature dropped after sunset and the stars came out like jewels spread out over black velvet. All she had was a light poncho in addition to her BDU shirt and undershirt. The days were still in the low nineties and they were dressed for the heat of the day, not the cold of night. Once the shaking stopped, she felt at one with the cold. By morning, she had never been so glad to feel the warm sunlight on her face and hands.

The laptop bleeped and she was shaken out of her remembrance. Shemp had responded to her question.

<shemp>   The poets.

She read it again; to be sure she had not imagined it. The poets. She felt a chill as she sat up in the kitchen chair. What were the odds that he would respond like that? She wanted to type her questions about the modern poets that were discussed on the radio, but she knew she could not give herself away.

<nooblet>   I say the coders.

<shemp>   Same difference. Some of the best programmers are not that different from poets.

<nooblet>   Code poets. LOL

There was a popular T-shirt with that message printed on it. Dancia always wanted one, but never had actually purchased it yet.

<shemp>   Yes, actually. There is a recognizable correlation between coding and writing poetry. Have you ever heard of Sun Microsystems

Richard Gabriel?

<nooblet> No.

<shemp>   He's a Distinguished Engineer who also writes a poem a day. He's even got a Master of Fine Arts degree. Granted, he's not from our generation, but he is a fine example of how the two skills are related.

Dancia thought about that for a moment. When she was in high school, she had written a few poems about her boyfriends and other typical teen angst. She had never tried to express herself in that way after graduation. Life in the military during a war did not afford her much free time for self-reflection.

<nooblet> I suppose the creativity is similar. The best coders have a flair for programming that you can't get in school or from a book.

<shemp>   Exactly. Well, I'm going to lie down for a while, before the sun comes up. Laters.

<nooblet> Where you at anyway?

<shemp>   Canada. You?

Dancia smiled. "I bet you speak French Canadian too." she said aloud to herself. She decided to be vague and give a trite answer.

<nooblet> The beautiful south.

<shemp>   Ha! Good band. G'nite.

She closed the laptop and turned the radio off before getting up and turning off the lights. It felt to her as if the apartment was on the cold side. She checked the thermostat on the way back to Joshua's room. It was set to sixty-five, no wonder she was chilled.

Unix was already snoring on the back of the couch and did not hear her flip the lights out when she left the room.

She came into his bedroom and watched him sleeping under a down comforter. He looked peaceful and warm. They hadn't discussed sleeping arrangements when they came back to his place and she really didn't care to stay on the couch. She peeled off her clothes and slid into the bed beside him. He didn't even stir. She pulled the covers up over her shoulders and waited for the flannel sheets to warm her up. She fell asleep before she noticed that she was warm.

CHAPTER 13

IT WAS A little past noon when Joshua awoke. It was the first time he had slept for more than a few hours in as many days. He felt rested and refreshed. He was on his side and looking across the room when he felt the presence of someone else in bed. The steady rhythmic motion of someone breathing beside him caused him to open both eyes wide and slowly turn over.

It was Dancia. She was lying on her side facing away from him. Wearing only her underwear! Joshua's mind raced. *Did they hook up last night?* He could not remember anything happening; surely he would have remembered something like that. He started thinking about what happened last night, going over everything in his mind. After a few minutes he realized that he was panicking for no reason. He had come to bed by himself.

Why was she in bed then? Perhaps she was tired and cold. He thought about that for a moment. Usually, when she spent the night at his apartment, she slept on his couch, like all his other friends did -- his guy friends anyway. She had never done anything this brazen before. Perhaps she was trying to tell him something. Perhaps she was hoping that something would happen. His heart started racing again. He really liked Dancia as a friend and he wanted to keep her as his friend. If they slept with each other; they would be more than just friends, they would be lovers. He was not ready to be her lover. Not until he figured out who was trying to kill them.

It was kind of weird, but he felt as though he were on a
mission to find the murderer and anything he did for himself,
only got in the way of that mission. He never realized that he
could be so committed to anything like that before; then again
his life was never threatened like it was now. He felt like he was
acting as some kind of Dudley Do Right. Not that he was ever
more than a straight arrow kind guy before, it's just that he never
really cared that much about anyone other than himself. He did
his own thing and if someone was into that, then he let them
come along, otherwise, he didn't care what they did as long as
they didn't get in his way. For now, a relationship with Dancia
would be getting in his way.

She began to stir and rolled over on her side facing him,
he rolled over on his back and watched her sleep. He used to
watch his old girlfriend sleep all the time. Lindsey was not a
morning person. She liked to sleep in as late as possible on
weekends. He was a morning person and would always wake up
before her and sometimes he would just lie in bed and watch her
sleep. She was so peaceful and content when she slept. So was
Dancia. Her breathing was calm and her black hair fell loosely
across her face covering an eye and part of her mouth. Lindsey
was a brunette and her hair was much longer and thinner than
Dancia's.

He had not thought about Lindsey in a few days, ever since
Glenn had died. Which was a good thing, he reckoned. They had
split several months ago under less than favorable circumstances
and he had not even seen her in passing since that time. She
was a career woman climbing the corporate ladder and she felt
that he was holding her back. He was not ready to commit to
marriage and she was not willing to ride along in a relationship
with no clear purpose other than to just be together. She needed
a husband to get to the next rung of the ladder and he was not the
man for the job. She dumped him and he didn't put up much of
a fight.

But he continued to think about her off and on for weeks after they split. The fact that he had not thought about her in a few days was a good sign. It meant that he was starting to get over her and get on with his life. He always knew that she was not the one for him, but sometimes when you are with someone for a long time, you find it hard to let them out of your life. He often wondered where she was, what she was doing; who she was with, but it never gave him any satisfaction thinking about her. It was not worth his time and energy and he knew that eventually he would stop thinking about her and move on. In that respect, the time he spent figuring out who killed Glenn and Zemo was therapeutic for him.

Dancia's eyes fluttered open and she looked up at Joshua, watching her. He smiled down at her and she pulled the covers up and managed an embarrassed grin.

"Good morning," Joshua said.

"I'm sorry, I just didn't feel like spending the night on your couch."

"Not a problem."

"Are you sure?" she asked, adjusting the covers and trying not to be exposed.

"You sleep like an angel; I didn't realize you were there right away."

She became defensive. "Nothing happened last night, I can assure you."

"Too bad," Joshua said, with a warm laugh.

Dancia looked at him oddly. Joshua saw the look and decided to get back to the business at hand. "Did you hear anything useful on the radio last night?"

She pushed the cover against her chest and sat up to face him. "Yes! I was listening to two guys talking French. They were having a very interesting conversation about Beatnik poetry. After they signed off, I found our man Shemp online in the chat room. I think he was one of the men I heard on the radio and he mentioned he was from Canada."

Joshua sat up while she was talking and his dark eyes narrowed as he listened to her.

"Canada. Did you write down their call signs?"

She nodded. "They are on your lappy desktop. I didn't think to look them up."

Joshua flung back the comforter and slid out of bed. He was wearing boxers as he padded down the hall and snagged the laptop from the kitchen table. Unix was standing at his water bowl. Joshua reached down and pet the cat's back and was rewarded with a quiet purr. He came back to bed with the laptop and slid under the warm blanket.

"Damn cold this morning."

"You mean this afternoon," she corrected him.

He opened the computer and added the first call sign, W5ZPGC, to the search box in his browser. Then he selected a browser search engine that Steve had written that let him search the FCC database for Amateur Radio call signs.

The results came back empty. He searched for inactive call signs only. Bingo. It was registered to a man in Florida who was listed as a silent key - meaning he had passed away. It was doubtful that Dancia was listening to a dead man talk last night. Something fishy was going on.

He entered the second license, which was the call sign - VE2SHM. It came back with Mike Metz, from Trois-Riviers Canada. Dancia glanced over his shoulder at the return.

"See, I bet that's our man Shemp. He said he was from Canada last night on IRC."

"Did you write down what band you heard them on?"

Dancia shook her head. "No, but the radio is still on frequency. It was a little lower than the number we got from IRC."

"Must have been a code for another band or something, I guess we can just keep it there and listen again tonight."

Dancia nodded. She lay back down and covered up. "I have to go back to work tonight. Are you staying up to listen? I heard them around three in the morning."

Joshua nodded, laid back and pulled the covers up over his chest. "I wonder if they are both up that late on a work night. Maybe if I listen as late as I can, I'll hear them earlier tonight. Heck, they may only talk on certain days of the week. It's going to be hit and miss."

Dancia sighed. "I'm not sure Shemp is capable of killing. He doesn't strike me as someone who is psychopathic. Actually, neither man sounded crazy in any way to me."

"I know what you mean. But maybe that's why no one has suspected them. I've been thinking about a motive for the murders and try as I might, I can't find anything about the two victims that someone would want to kill them over. They were programmers but aside from that, they had little in common, except being a member of our web project.

"One was a brilliant coder and the other one was not. One was a loved member of the community and the other was just a middle aged corporate hack. Neither one talked to the other on IRC that we know of. I could find no emails between them or even between Shemp and them."

Dancia yawned. "Maybe the killer doesn't want us to go public."

Joshua had no idea how the mind of a crazy person worked. It may be that he didn't have to have any connection to them, but somehow that did not feel right. Something inside Joshua was telling him it was another programmer. He was so convinced of it, he refused to even consider anyone else.

"I think he's a programmer and I think he wants to kill us because we are programmers," Joshua said.

"The killer needed someone to be at their computer in order to strike. Computer geeks are always at their computers. He also needed them to be online and using headphones. Again, what coder doesn't have a broadband connection and listen to music?"

She stared at the ceiling and scrunched her face as she figured. "So we're looking for a programmer who likes to kill other programmers?" There was a note of disbelief in her tone.

"It sounds weak, but that's because we just don't have a motive," Joshua insisted.

They lay there in silence, both of them thinking.

"Maybe he's trying to prove himself," Joshua said, breaking the silence. "Like a hotshot kid who wants to show how l33t his skills are."

Dancia looked at him, a sly grin spreading on her face. "Killing someone with code would be a pretty bold statement for a cocky young coder."

Joshua agreed. "The ultimate hack." They were both well steeped in Hacker lore and they knew how common it was for new Hackers to feel the need to prove themselves. Traditionally, it was pulling off a technically difficult prank on someone or some group, but lately it was more about writing an application that other Hackers used or admired for its technical excellence and its creative elegance.

This was not to be confused with writing programs that defaced web sites or that let script kiddies hack into school computers or data centers, that was cracking and most real Hackers were as far removed from that behavior as you could get. A Hacker was someone who was at a different level of skill and understanding.

Dancia winced. "How are we going to prove that to the police? They don't know anything about Hacker culture."

"We just have to find out more about how he managed to kill them and hope that we turn up something damning on Shemp. I still have issues with using Flash animation to hypnotize someone. Unless he was talking to his victim through the headsets they wore and was able to offer spoken suggestions."

Dancia turned to face him. "Wouldn't he have to know what the person was afraid of in order to use that to kill them?"

"Maybe we can look for something in the chat logs about fears or phobias? I still got a problem with the motivation thing. Proving yourself by killing seems very brutal even for a nut job programmer. There has to be some kind of a connection between our group and the killer."

Dancia agreed with a nod. Joshua got out of the bed headed for his dresser. "Lets get clean and have some breakfast then we can get to work on finding a motive."

/*---*/

After his shower Joshua headed to the kitchen to start the pancakes and more importantly, the coffee pot. As he waited for the griddle to warm up, he pushed the oil around making sure to cover the whole cooking surface. His mom had first taught him to make pancakes when he was six years old. He was too short to reach the stove, so she let him stand on a footstool. It was one of the first times he remembered cooking with his mother - something the two of them would do a lot of as he grew up. She was a fine cook and loved to improve her craft by watching cooking shows and making new dishes every once in a while. Joshua's dad was always ready with a technical explanation of why things were done the way they were in the kitchen, but his mom tended to cook on instinct. She could make just about anything in the kitchen and her instincts were passed on to her son who found that cooking relaxed him and gave him a creative outlet that was outside the world of bits and bytes.

There was knocking at the door and Joshua knew by the sound that it was Tripp. He unlocked the door and Tripp entered, his nose immediately smelling the coffee and the heating oil. "Pancakes for lunch?" he asked.

"Yeah, well, it was a long night."

Tripp came into the kitchen and noticed the big radio on the kitchen table. "What's with the antique?"

"I was listening for someone to talk on the Ham bands last night. It's a long story. What are you up to today?"

Tripp stood beside him at the stove, looking around at the two plates and two coffee cups set out. He looked at Joshua who seemed not to notice anything wrong.

"Were you expecting company?" he asked, nodding to the counter.

Joshua tried to come up with an explanation that would satisfy his curious friend.

"Sure smells good in here," Dancia stated before she came into the kitchen and saw Tripp.

Tripp's eyes bugged out as he immediately put the clues together. She was wearing a towel on her head and one of Joshua's long sleeve T-shirts that read, "Code Monkey".

"Oh, hi Tripp. Joshua, do you happen to have a hair dryer?"

"Sure, in the cabinet under the sink."

"Thanks, tootles," she teased as she headed back down the hall towards the master bedroom. Both men stared at her bare legs as she strode down the hall.

Tripp and Joshua exchanged looks. "You dog, you finally hooked up with her!"

"No, really. That's not what happened."

"Right, dude. She's wearing your clothes and using your bathroom." Tripp slapped his friend on the back and started to head for the door. "I'll leave you love birds alone. Catch you later man."

"Tripp, don't go. It's not what you think, really. I have plenty of pancakes. Please, stay."

Tripp paused, the pancakes did smell pretty good and he hadn't had any lunch yet. Joshua flipped the pancakes on the griddle. "Grab a plate and sit down."

You didn't have to bend his arm to get Tripp to eat. He turned around and came back to the kitchen.

"Alright, but I feel like a third wheel."

"Don't. Nothing happened, we were working late last night and I offered to let her use the shower."

Tripp motioned to the radio. "What's got you two so busy, not getting busy, anyway?"

Joshua poured four more pancakes on the griddle and handed Tripp a plate with the first batch on it. Tripp helped himself to a fork and brought the butter plate and syrup to the table.

Joshua poured Tripp and himself a cup of coffee. "Remember those programmers that died Friday?"

Tripp nodded as he stuffed a fork full of pancakes in his mouth. The sound of Joshua's old hair dryer came from the back bathroom.

"They were murdered. I found evidence on Glenn's computer that someone killed him. It's a bit complicated, but it looks like the killer used a program to somehow hypnotize Glenn and then kill him at his computer."

Tripp listened intently as he chewed. "Have you gone to the police yet?"

"No, I wanted to give myself the weekend to look through his computers and see if I could ascertain who might have gotten on his system. I don't think the police have much of a computer crimes department. If I can get a suspect and or a good motive, I'll go in and tell them what I know. Until then, we really don't have much of a case."

"Still, you better be careful, messing with evidence."

"I have not modified his system, just copied some log files. Technically, it's not a crime until the case is declared a murder. Either way, I think we are on the trail of someone, so it may not be too much longer before we find out who it was and inform the police. If I'm right, the killer may be wanted for both murders."

Tripp smiled. "Maybe you should be going to the CIA or Interpol or something. You could be on the trail of an international terrorist."

Joshua slid the next batch on a plate and poured some more pancakes on the griddle. "Maybe, but until we catch our man in some incriminating way, we don't have anything."

"Who is your suspect?"

Dancia came back into the kitchen. "Some hacker named Shemp." Her black hair was freshly styled and she smelled soapy clean.

Tripp looked at her and stopped chewing. "His name is Shemp?"

"No, that's his alias, his real name is Mike Metz and he's from Canada. Thanks," she said, taking a plate full of pancakes from Joshua. She sat down at the table opposite Tripp.

"I don't think he's your man," Tripp said.

Joshua turned around. "Why do you say that?"

"Shemp was one of the three stooges."

Joshua and Dancia exchanged looks of astonishment. Dancia smiled, she knew Shemp was not the one. Joshua looked back at Tripp. "Curly, Moe and Larry. Who was Shemp?"

"He was one of the original stooges, but he left the group before they became famous. They replaced him with Curly."

Joshua looked back at the griddle and watched as the tiny bubbles formed in the pancakes he just poured. If Shemp was a "Stooge" then who was controlling him? He tried to remember the conversation on IRC when they first started monitoring it late Saturday night. Who was the older guy that everyone considered a Perl guru? Muse.

"It's Muse, he's the killer. He's using Shemp as his stooge."

Tripp swallowed and brought his fork up to point at Joshua. "Who's Muse?"

"Another participant in an IRC chat room we've been monitoring," Dancia said. She had stopped eating and was thinking about that first night. "He was someone that the other guys all respected because he was a Perl guru."

Tripp continued eating while he spoke. "Always there is an

apprentice and a master. Sounds like you guys were going after the apprentice."

Joshua grinned; Tripp was always ready with a nerdy *Star Wars* quote. Sometimes hanging out with him was like being in a Kevin Smith movie. You never knew when he would launch into a lengthy dissertation on why Han shot first. At least he didn't try to sound like Yoda - this time.

Joshua turned off the stove and flipped his serving of pancakes onto a plate. He covered them with butter and then poured some maple syrup on them. He ate standing up, and facing his friends. He sipped his cup of coffee between bites.

He and Dancia exchanged glances, now they had to look for a connection between Zemo, Themis, Dancia, Joshua and Shemp.

Tripp finished eating. He stood up and brought his plate to the sink, letting Joshua sit down at the table. "Well kids, it's been interesting, but I have to be going."

"Where you off to?" Joshua asked.

"Gotta make a quick stop off at the Flying M to pick up Dave and then we're off to a movie. I was going to see if you wanted to come with us, but you guys are busy playing Clue."

"Can you drop off Dancia at her place? She doesn't have her car."

Dancia finished her last bite and brought her plate to the sink.

"Sure, no problem."

CHAPTER 14

<shemp>	No, I have never met Muse. Why do you ask?
<nooblet>	I was just curious how old he was. He seems to come off as one of those longhaired, bearded types in tie died T-shirts and sandals.
<shemp>	LOL
<mostaban>	Yes, he lives in his cube at his office and showers in the men's room.
<nooblet>	Don't laugh, I used to know a guy like that at my last job. He was a UNIX hippy. Not all there upstairs sometimes, but he sure as shit knew his way around the file system.
<shemp>	Muse is not like that. He's pretty much a normal guy like any of us.

Dancia smiled. *What a stooge, he even protects his master.* She was sitting on the floor in her room, still wearing Joshua's T-shirt, with a hoodie over it to keep her arms warm. Her laptop was running Gentoo Linux. Gentoo was a custom Linux distribution that was favored by system administrators because it let you build nearly everything from scratch, thereby making the software conform to the hardware like a fitted T-shirt to a body.

It was getting close to the diner hour and she was starting to get hungry. She was due back on shift in a couple hours, but she really didn't want to go in. She was having too much fun chatting with her new Perl buddies and trying to find a motive for which one was a killer. Muse was not in the chat room so they all felt comfortable with talking about him.

<nooblet>   So just how good a coder is Muse anyway? What has he done that would garner the kind of loyalty you guys all have for him?

<mostaban>   He's never not had an answer for any problem we have had.   You know he knows his shit. He's a national treasure for what he knows.

<losing>   The guy really knows programming.   He's an old school Hacker.

<shemp>   He was in Nam, towards the end during the pull out.   He has seen some bad shit.   But he never talks about it, at least not to any of us.   I found a post he wrote on a Veteran's board once about living with the bad memories.

<mostaban>   I didn't know he was in Nam.

<shemp>   Like I said, he never talks about it.

<nooblet>   I was in the sandbox.   I've seen some shit.   Not something I talk about either.

<shemp>   Really? Army or Marines?

<nooblet>   Never mind.

<losing>   Nooblet, you don't have to talk about it man. Just know that we all appreciate what you did.

<mostaban>   Not everyone has the balls to go fight for their country. Thanks man!

Dancia swallowed hard. She had never talked about her military career since getting out. In many ways it was like a bad dream but she did appreciate the kind sentiments of most people when they found out she had served in Iraq. The experience had hardened her to the dark side of human nature. It had forced her to see the good and the bad in herself and her fellow Marines. Her way of dealing with it was to try and forget it, even though she knew that those experiences would be forever with her and had changed her for better or worse. She knew that people were capable of doing some pretty horrific things and that kind of scared her sometimes.

Her own war experience had given her a new found respect for older war veterans. She no longer looked at them as freaks or as damaged goods for what they had been through. She didn't want recognition in the form of medals or coverage in the press, she just wanted to live her life to it's fullest and never have to be in a situation where she was forced to take life and to be staring at death's face again until she was very old.

<shemp>   None of us have even been in the military.

<nooblet>   What else can you tell me about muse? Where does he live?

<mostaban>   Montana or Colorado maybe. I heard him mention some mountains and sage brush around his place once.

<shemp>   Somewhere in the American West. He's pretty tight lipped about exactly where. Where do you live Nooblet?

Dancia hesitated; she didn't want to let them know exactly where she was either. She tried to think of someplace that she knew well enough to lie convincingly about. She had never lived anywhere but Idaho and a few Marine bases. She decided to be evasive.

<nooblet>   Western US. I'm trying not to let the world know how cool my home town is, so that nobody will want to come here. Know what I mean?

<mostaban>   Ha. I know what you mean.

<shemp>   You Yanks can come up to the Great White North.

<nooblet>   Where are you at in Canada, Shemp?

<shemp>   Central Canada, Tri-Rivers area. It's an old town with lots of history and beautiful buildings.

We   get   plenty   of   tourists,   especially   for   the
festival.

<mostaban>   Don't   even   get   him   started   on   poetry.   Hey
Nooblet,   heard   any   news   on   that   German   kid
who died?

Dancia took her fingers off the keyboard and stared at the chat
window. Nobody had talked about that before in this channel,
at least not when she was on. She wondered if Mostaban was a
stooge too or maybe he was actually Muse. Maybe they were
all in on it and she was the stooge. No way, she was letting her
imagination get the best of her. She put her hands back on the
keyboard and started to type.

<nooblet>   What German kid?

<mostaban>   Are   you   kidding   me?   Everyone   knows   about
Zemo   getting   murdered   at   his   computer   last
week.

<nooblet>   Oh   yeah,   I   think   I   saw   something   on   Digg   about
that.

<mostaban>   The   police   think   he   was   murdered,   but   they
can't   find   any   suspect   and   they   don't   have   a
clue how it was done.

<nooblet>   Sounds fishy to me.

<mostaban>   I   think   he   was   killed   by   a   Hacker;   someone
who   can   kill   with   code,   like   some   kind   of
mutant from the X-Men or something.

<shemp>   Mostaban,   you're   a   nerd.   You   can't   kill
someone   with   code;   this   is   reality   here.   Put
away the comic books.

<nooblet>   What kind of dork are you anyway?

<mostaban>   Whatever,   but   I   can't   see   any   other   way   to
reach   through   someone's   computer   and   kill
them.

<nooblet>   I'm   sure   the   police   will   find   something.   No
crime goes unpunished.

\<shemp\>   Eventually the grim reaper gets all.

There he goes, evading the topic and adding a dramatic flare. She slid the laptop to the floor and stretched her arms. Her cell phone started playing a jazzy tune from her pocket.

"Hello."

"Dancia, you going into work tonight?"

It was Joshua. She loved the sound of his voice.

"Yeah."

"Me too, in the morning. I'm going to listen to the short wave as late as I can, see if I can catch them chatting again."

"But they talk in French, how are you going to know what they are talking about?"

"I won't. I'll record them and let you listen to it later and translate it."

Oh, well there's a thought. She wanted to come over to his place and hang out until she had to go in. But she was having trouble thinking up a good excuse to come over.

"Have you been monitoring IRC?"

"No, been doing laundry and listening to the radio."

"Have you had diner yet?" It was just after seven in the evening.

"No, you?"

"No. I'm coming over." She decided to just be forward and not explain anything.

"Okay."

She packed a book bag with a change of clothes and some makeup and her toothbrush and threw it in her KG before leaving. She didn't want to be caught without it again. On the short drive over, she stopped at the pizzeria behind the Flying M coffee house and got a medium pie to go.

They ate the pizza at the kitchen table, while they listened to the radio and talked. Joshua opened some beers for them.

"I learned that Muse is a Vietnam veteran. Shemp offered that tidbit this afternoon," Dancia offered.

"Really? I suppose we should be putting together a psychological work-up on the guy to try and find out what would make him a murderer. I never took any psychology classes in college."

"I did. Not that that makes me any kind of expert. Let's see, we know he's in his fifties, possibly early sixties to have been in that conflict. Everyone in that room thinks very highly of him and his hacker skills. So he's probably been in the IT field since its origins."

Joshua finished chewing. "So he prolly started on main frames. Man, I can't even imagine living in those days."

Dancia smiled, she couldn't either. They thought they had it bad on a 486-based chip in the early nineties. "Neither can I. I tried to paint a portrait of him as some kind of Berkley hippie, but Shemp shot me down. He insists that Muse is a normal guy like any of them. But still, how would he know for sure, he's never met Muse?"

Joshua thought about that for a moment. If they have been chatting on Ham radio, and in a chat room, they may indeed know each other pretty well and still never have met in person. Like two people who meet online and get to know each other with intentions of meeting in person and getting married. Many times they think they really know the person and then when they finally meet, the other person has an annoying personal habit that never came out in correspondence and the marriage is called off.

"I don't know, maybe Shemp is lying. Maybe they have met and he's trying not to let anyone know."

Dancia remembered something "Oh, Shemp said he was from the Tri-Rivers area of Canada. Let's look that up and see what we can find. Nobody seemed to know exactly where Muse lived, other than out West."

"Did you tell them where you lived?"

"Nope."

Joshua wiped his hands on a napkin and left the table to get his MacBook. When he returned, she had made a space for him to set it down next to her. He moved his chair around and sat down, opening the laptop. He opened Firefox and typed the Canadian city into the Wikipedia search box. She helped him spell it, as it was a French word. Trois-Riviers sits at the confluence of the three prongs of the Saint Maurice and the Saint Lawrence Rivers in Quebec. They both read the Wikipedia article in silence, neither one of them had been to Canada.

"International Poetry Capital of the World?" Joshua intoned. They both looked at each other. Shemp was talking about poetry to the other guy on the radio.

"Perhaps our Muse is really a muse," Dancia stated. "I would have to say there is a strong possibility that they have met at this festival on at least one occasion."

Joshua nodded in thought. "We should see what we can find about a poet that goes by the name Muse."

Dancia glanced at the kitchen clock and then back to Joshua. "I have to get to work. You going to google Muse then?"

"Go ahead. If you get bored tonight, you can monitor the IRC and do some searches."

She helped him clean up the pizza and beer before she left. Joshua appreciated her help and he told her to stop by when she got off work, he would be going in a little later this week so they could compare notes. After she left, he sat down at the radio and tuned around for a while. He didn't hear anything so he retired to his computer room for a few hours of googling.

The first thing he did was write a program. A small Ruby script that parsed a Wikipedia page for words that were links and then searched Wikipedia for all the definitions found on the single page. The program kicked out a simple text file with all the definitions found on a single Wikipedia page. The file was updated whenever the Wikipedia page was altered. It actively polled the live page and adjusted its results in real time. It didn't have to be that elaborate, but once he started writing the script, he could not finish until it was the best he could make it.

Two hours later, he hit the Muse article on Wikipedia and within seconds had a text file with all the many definitions of Muse found on the page. Then he set about doing searches on each word that interested him. He briefly thought about adding a search engine parser to the script, but realized that he would be programming more than actually trying to find what he was looking for - a connection behind any of the names of the Muses with a programmer whose hacker handle was Muse.

He took a break and went back into the kitchen for a drink of water. While he was filling his glass, he heard the radio come alive with conversation. It was Shemp and Muse; he knew it because they were speaking French. Following Amateur Radio protocol, they said their call signs in English.

Joshua scrambled to get his digital tape player and started recording as he sat down and listened. He had very little clue as to what they were saying, but he could tell that Muse was coming in much louder. He wondered if Muse was closer to him. She did say that he lived out West; maybe he was real close. That thought was not too comforting.

Joshua turned the fine tuner knob to see if he could bring in the signals better. He was having trouble hearing Shemp due to a wavering signal that seemed to fade in and out. An idea occurred to him as he found a cleaner signal. He wondered if Steve could some how locate Muse's signal. Steve used to talk about doing something called Fox Hunts using his Ham radio gear. A bunch of guys with special antennas would drive around town looking for a hidden transmitter using triangulation and signal strength meters. *Could something like that be done with High Frequency signals?*

He pulled out his cell phone and dialed Steve's number.

"Hello."

"Steve, this is Joshua. Is it possible to locate a HF signal?

You know like when you do those Fox Hunts?"

"Well, those are done using VHF or UHF signals, much closer to home. I suppose one could do something similar on HF, but you would need to have many Hams located all around the country or the world to isolate the signal. Even then you would most likely just be able to get the general area down to a few states."

Joshua dropped his shoulders. "Oh."

"Are you listening to your suspect?"

"Yeah right on the same frequency."

"Is one of them coming in more powerful than the other for you?"

Steve was silent for a moment as he dialed in the frequency on his fancy modern rig. "Yep, but sometimes when conditions are bad, like right now, signal strength is not a reliable indicator of how close a signal is to you. Radio is kind of fickle in that way. He is coming in a solid S9. He could be local."

"Do you mean local as in state or city?"

"Either."

Joshua sighed. "He's using a bogus call sign. I looked it up and it's from a silent key."

"Really? We could turn him in to the FCC, but it would be difficult to find out whom he really is. That whole process could take a while to resolve. His voice sounds funny to me. Like he's talking through some kind of..."

"What?" Joshua asked.

"I think he's masking his voice through a filter of some kind. Notice how he sounds like a really fat robot?"

Joshua was not sure if it were normal behavior for HF signals or not. "I did notice that."

"I bet he's using some kind of electronic voice scrambler, like they use on TV when a victim does not want to be identified."

"That would fit. He's using multiple methods to mask his identity."

Steve sighed. "Damn idiot. People like him give Ham Radio a bad name."

"Yeah well, he's done more than break a few radio rules. He's also a killer."

"Right. You going to the police in the morning?"

"Yes. I just hope I can give them enough information to find this slime ball."

"Good luck man. I gotta get to bed."

"Me too, thanks Steve."

"No problem, later."

Joshua put the phone down and continued to listen to the radio. They talked for another ten minutes before signing off. Joshua turned off the recorder and then shut down the radio. He padded back to his room and went to bed. It was a little past midnight when he dozed off. Within an hour he was awake again tormented by the car accident. He lay in his bed and tried to forget the terrible images by reading Cory Doctorow's *Little Brother*.

CHAPTER 15

JOSHUA SLAPPED THE snooze bar three times then noticed he was late and rushed into the shower. He could shave, brush teeth, relieve himself, shower and dress in under 30 minutes. This morning Nix had pooped all over the floor in the hallway, so he lost some time cleaning that mess. The thought occurred to him again to get rid of the poor old animal, but he knew he could not do it. He usually didn't bother eating breakfast just grabbed a coffee at a drive through place on his way into work.

It was a Monday and it was his first day back at work after Glenn's death. The traffic was light to moderate heading West through Garden City. He was lucky to live down town because it meant he was commuting against the flow of traffic into Boise. He had enough time to guzzle most of his coffee before cruising into the main gate at RegTech. It was just after eight and the parking lot was full. He had to park farther out from his building, which made for a cold walk on a crisp, sunny morning. The wind was blowing harder than usual from the West, which meant a front was moving in from the Pacific coast. He noticed the high stratus clouds and understood that rain or snow was less than forty-eight hours away.

He thought about heading out to the airport after work and messing around with his dad's Cessna 120. He liked to work on it whenever he needed to think something through. Cleaning the grease and bugs off the classic plane seemed to relax his mind and let him think without any distractions. There was no Internet, no friends popping by and no phones, provided he turned his cell off, which he frequently did while he was in the hangar. He pushed thoughts about the airplane from his head, hard as that was. He had to get back into the swing of things and focus on his work. There would be many distractions today and he knew it would be tough to concentrate.

Walking up to the outside door of building four he swiped his security badge and opened the glass door. He felt like everyone in the building was looking at him even though hardly anyone paid him any attention at all. When he got to his row, he slowed down as he passed Glenn's cube. There it was, empty and clean. Just two days before it had been the home of someone who worked here, now it was just another empty cube, soon to be occupied by another person. Any evidence of who used to work in the space would be gone forever. He thought about the transitory nature of work cubes and how many different people had lived in each cube over the years. There was really very little of Glenn left behind in his cube. His spirit survived in the code that he had written, but even that would no doubt change over time and at some point be completely thrown out for the latest technology.

Information workers rarely had anything substantial or real that you could hold in your hands and say, 'I worked on this item and a little bit of my soul is inside of it.' More often then not, there were only temporary bits and bytes of information that could be lost forever with a stroke of a key or a random hardware failure. At least an Architect could point to a building and say that he designed it. Although, time and nature could render that building a pile of rubble just as easily as any careless user could destroy a code file. That thought made Joshua realize that what he did was not always as fleeting as it seemed.

He put his book bag down in his cube, sat down and turned

on his PC. While he waited for it to boot up, he picked up his phone and listened to a couple voice mail messages waiting for him. One was from RegTech Security, reminding him to come down and sign something; he didn't really care about the details. Two more were from coworkers expressing their sorrow for Glenn's untimely passing. The phone messages got him in a down mood, so he dug his iPod out and dialed up some happy tunes. He sat and listened to "In the Garage" by *Weezer*, as he read through his emails and opened the programs he always used. By the time he finished getting organized he was ready for a break and a fresh cup of coffee. He locked his PC and picked up his cup that still had old coffee from Friday in it. On his way to the coffee station, he stepped into the men's room to wash it out.

As he was rinsing the cup, someone came out of the stall and nodded to him. It was Larry Taggert, the UNIX guy from a few rows over. Taggert never said much to anyone and Joshua didn't expect him to say anything now. Joshua wiped out the cup with a brown paper towel as Taggert washed his hands.

"Didn't your supervisor give you some time off?"

Joshua looked up. "Huh? Oh, yeah, but I'm all right. Besides, I've got some work to keep me busy."

Taggert looked at him with a concerned eye.

"You look tired. Have you been getting enough sleep?"

"I'm fine."

Taggert nodded and managed a thin smile. "Take it easy then."

"Thanks," Joshua said. He ducked out of the room and headed down the hall. *That was weird.* Guy never speaks a word to him in years and then out of the blue is all concerned for him. Maybe he felt he should look after Joshua having been a friend of Joshua's father years before. Joshua figured the whole day was going to be like that, uncomfortable encounters with coworkers until everyone had said their condolences.

He filled up his cup with fresh java and dumped a couple packs of sugar and a creamer in it. While he was stirring his coffee another coworker came up and offered her condolences. It was Stacy Grimes, the Copywriter on the web team. She was a bit mousy and wore wire-rimmed glasses. She hid behind straight brown hair that dropped in front of her eyes when she looked down, which see seemed to always be doing. She was painfully shy, but she knew grammar rules better than anyone he had ever known.

"Sorry about Glenn. You doing okay Joshua?"

"I'm okay. You?"

She looked up at him briefly, as if nobody ever asked her how she felt about anything. She nodded, and then quickly went back to her cube. Joshua walked back to his cube and avoided eye contact with anyone. He turned his music on again and sipped his coffee. His mind wandered as he looked over the code he had been writing on Friday, before the interruption.

He thought about how someone would write a Flash program that could hypnotize a viewer. Technically, the mechanics of Flash allowed for just about any moving image to be manipulated with underlying code. But you would have to be familiar with the technique of hypnotizing before you could design such a program. That got him thinking about what qualified someone to be a hypnotist. *Did you take classes? Learn at someone's side, like an apprentice?* He did not know. Obviously, if the killer used that technique, he not only knew how to code Flash but also how to hypnotize someone.

Joshua opened a browser and started searching for anything on Flash and hypnosis. While exploring, he found that virtually anyone can learn to hypnotize themselves or others. Experts recommended that you learn from certified individuals and that you only use the condition to help improve yourself or others. He wondered what damage could be done to someone under hypnosis if your intent was to harm instead of to help.

He searched for examples of people dying as a result of being hypnotized and came up empty. Either it was not easy to do, or people did not want to admit that it was possible to avoid further injuries.

His search stretched out for hours and he realized that he was getting very little work done. Then he came across a reference for something called Binaural Beat music. When the brain is presented with two beats that were below 1000 Hz and they differed no more than 30 Hz, the two beats combined and became a binaural beat that could put the brain into an altered state. This altered state, can then be used to hypnotize someone. Joshua slowly began to make connections about how Glenn and Zemo could have become hypnotized. Both of them were wearing earmuff style headphones that had the added ability to isolate them from back ground noise. If they were subjected to this binaural beat music they could have been slowly hypnotized without even realizing it. They may not have even needed a visual stimulus.

If that were the case, then Muse would not have to be a Flash programmer at all. Either that, or if he did use Flash in the seduction, it may have only helped to move the victim into a more suggestive state quicker than with only the music. He thought about that for a while. Muse would have to have possessed detailed knowledge of music and electronics to create the binaural beats. They already know that Muse was into Ham radio, which still required its participants to understand at least basic circuitry if not advanced theories about sound wave propagation and creation. So theoretically Muse would have enough know how to pull off hypnotizing someone. The only thing missing was just exactly how he was able to kill them.

Joshua could not even imagine how hypnotized people could allow themselves to die. Everything he had read suggested that the patients being hypnotized would never allow themselves to do anything that they were morally averse to doing while conscious.

Joshua googled some more for possible deadly side effects of hypnotizing a person, sifting through the returns with care and found another interesting tidbit. But it had nothing to do with hypnosis. He came across a study about death from fright. Apparently, Air Force test pilots are routinely monitored for vital signs while they put new aircraft designs through their paces. Many pilots, while trapped in fatal dives were found to have their hearts stop beating moments before impact. They were literally scared to death before they died. Rapid amounts of endorphins pumped into the body during such traumatic events could cause heart failure.

Joshua stopped reading and sat back in his chair. *What if Muse was able to convince his victims that they were about to die? Could they have been frightened to death?* A cold chill ran through Joshua, causing goose flesh on his bare arms. *In order to pull that off Muse must have known what each person was most afraid of in such detail that he could suggest to them that their fears were real.* It still sounded far-fetched to Joshua, but he knew he was on to something.

Someone stood before the entrance to Joshua's cube, breaking him out of his thoughts. It was Nik Dean, a coder from the test team that played in a local metal band. Nik was a lean, longhaired guy dressed in torn jeans and a T-shirt that read "Me worry?". He also wore an old leather jacket that had seen better days. He was a drummer for the band and he always seemed to be moving, keeping time to life.

"What's sup?" Rik asked.

"Hey Nik, not much. You?"

Nik came inside Joshua's cube and plopped down in the guest chair. He seemed to occupy the chair like a spider would - all spread out with limbs bent over it.

"I guess our little break club just got smaller."

Joshua nodded. "You need a fix?"

"Yes, let's go."

They got up and headed down the rows of cubicles to the back entrance of the building. There was a designated smoking area tucked under the eve of an adjacent building. As soon as they were outside, Nik had lit up a cigarette and was puffing it as they walked over to the picnic table. Joshua stood upwind to avoid the smoke.

"I never figured anyone would die before me. You know, due to my insane lifestyle and all."

Joshua grinned. Nik was either drunk or high depending on what time of day it was. He was real good at keeping it clean at work, but the guy could party with the best rockers. Joshua had been to several of his gigs at local clubs and took an interest in what Nik had to say about his music and life in general. For a metal head, he was pretty deep at times. Joshua liked that about Nik. To look at him you would immediately label him a loser, but he was actually a centered individual who knew where he came from and where he wanted to go. Joshua respected that about him. He also loved the band's crazy fast drum solos that Nik pounded out with ease.

"Don't say anything to anyone, but I don't think Glenn died of a heart attack. I mean, he prolly died of heart failure, but I think it was induced by someone," Joshua said, after making sure nobody was around to hear them.

Nik got a serious look on his face as he took a drag.

"You think he was murdered?"

"Yup. You hear about that coder in Germany who died?"

"No."

Joshua could not believe someone did not know about that, but then Nik was only into coding at work. He was real good at it, but he never hung out in chat rooms or visited geek sites like Slashdot or Digg. He was more often playing games on his home PC or hanging out on his MySpace page, mixing it up with groupies of his band.

"This coder kid was found dead and the police ruled it murder because they found a calling card in his source code. It's all over the internet man."

Nik thought about it for a minute. "So, like you think Glenn was killed by the same guy?"

"I know it. I found the same message in the code he was working on the day he died."

Nik shook his head in disbelief. "Man that's messed up. You tell the cops yet?"

"No, I'm actually trying to figure out who did it first. I'm real close to figuring out how it was done and who did it. As soon as I know for sure, I'm going to the cops."

Nik walked around, tapping his foot to some unheard beat. He smashed his cigarette in the table and took out his pack to knock out another one. After tapping on the pack a few times he took a fresh one out and lit it with a Bic lighter.

"So, how do you think he was killed then?"

Joshua sat down on the table and put his feet on the seat. "I think they were hypnotized and then while they were under a trance, the killer convinced them that they were going to die. Maybe took advantage of some fear they each had. Made them think that they could not survive something. There is some evidence that fear will send large amounts of adrenaline to the heart, enough to stop it."

Nik started pointing for emphasis as he spoke. "I've heard of that man. You know what else it could have been?"

Joshua shook his head.

"Arrhythmia, the irregular heart beat. Certain snare drum rhythms have been know to cause people's hearts to get messed up. Some have died from it."

Joshua's face clearly displayed his disbelief. "That's an urban myth, has to be."

Nik shrugged. "I've heard it from many musicians."

Joshua grinned. "Whatever. Have you ever felt it?"

"No, but that's because I'm causing it. I've heard bassists and leads say they can feel it if they are near the bass speakers at a concert."

Joshua was not convinced, but he let it slide. Nik finished up his cancer stick and they walked back inside. Nik went back to his cube and Joshua loitered around the main hallway. *Should I go out somewhere or just settle for a cheeseburger at the campus choke and puke?* Neither sounded appetizing to him.

He strolled past Lawrence Taggert's cube and looked at the poster of the moon on his outer cube wall. There was something familiar about that moon poster. Then it hit him. It was the same poster that was behind Ed Asner's desk in that seventies sitcom *Mary Tyler Moore*. He forgot that Taggert was that old. Joshua's parents used to watch that show and he remembered seeing it on Cable TV not too long ago. As he was standing there lost in thought, Taggert came out of his cube.

"Hey man, what's up?"

Joshua stuttered. "Ah, I was just looking at this cool poster."

Taggert looked at the poster and then back to Joshua. "Your dad gave me that years ago. I think I must have said something about it one night when we were watching TV. A few weeks later he came in and handed it to me in a cardboard tube."

"Mary Tyler Moore. That was the TV show," Joshua offered.

Taggert squinted as if he were trying to recall the show. Then he lit up. "That was it. Ed Asner had it behind his desk."

They both nodded in agreement before falling into an awkward silence. Finally Taggert shook his head. "I used to think NASA stuff was pretty far out. Your dad did too. You know he even worked for NASA once?"

Far out. You don't hear that phrase much anymore.

"I remember him talking about it."

"He was too good for them. They knew it too. That's why he came here in the seventies and helped build RegTech. I followed him out here to the middle of nowhere. I should have stayed in the Sunshine state."

Joshua didn't really feel like traveling down memory lane. "Well, I have to go get some lunch. See you around, Larry."

Taggert nodded and started walking towards the cafeteria. Joshua went back to his cube and plopped down in his chair. He didn't feel like coding. He didn't feel like doing anything. He logged on and did some searches for snare drums causing arrhythmia. Nothing turned up, just like he figured. He probably should not have told Nik about the murder plot. He hoped his friend kept his mouth shut, at least for another day or so.

Joshua considered going to the police after lunch, but he just couldn't bring himself to do it until he knew who Muse was. It was starting to bother him more and more.

CHAPTER 16

JOSHUA THOUGHT ABOUT his dreams again as he found himself cruising into the subdivision where he used to live. Sometimes he drove by his old house and stared at it, remembering good times with his mom and dad; learning to plant flowers with his mom on a warm spring afternoon, throwing catch with his dad on the front lawn on a hot summer day and backing out of the driveway for his first driving lesson. The memories tended to make him smile and feel good inside as he drove past the older, two story house.

The house was well kept by the current owners and a fresh coat of paint in a new color kept it looking modern. He saw evidence of children in the yard; an electric Jeep, a soccer ball and colored chalk on the driveway. There was a station wagon in the garage and bicycles hanging from the same hooks that his dad installed for their bikes. It was somehow comforting to him that the house that was his home for most of his life was still someone's home today. It meant that he could return here whenever he wanted and see physical evidence of his own family's past existence.

As he drove slowly down the street he noticed that Tripp's dad was in his driveway cleaning out his truck. Greg Thomas saw him coming down the street and waved for him to stop. Joshua pulled into the driveway and got out of his car.

"Hey Joshua, what brings you out this way?"

"I was just in the area and thought I'd stop by."

Joshua shook the hand of his surrogate father. After his parents had died, Joshua lived with Tripp's family until he graduated high school and could legally take custody of his parent's estate. Greg Thomas was the closest thing to a father Joshua had and he stopped by to visit whenever he could.

"We just got back from a weekend in Sun Valley," Greg said.

Joshua grabbed a ski bag out of the truck and followed Greg into the garage with it. Greg was in his late fifties and retired from banking. He had thick salt and pepper hair and a mustache. His eyes were hazel behind wrinkled skin.

"Tripp tells me you are working on his movie web site again. How's that going?"

Joshua didn't want to worry his adopted family about what was going on. In a few days the danger would be over and his life would be back to normal. It didn't sound like Tripp had mentioned anything about the killings.

"It's going pretty good. We should be looking for backers in another month or so."

Greg looked surprised. "Really? Wow, sounds like you had better get working on your business plan."

Joshua smiled. *Greg always thought like a banker.*

"I will, I'll give you a call when we have a working beta."

Greg flashed a friendly smile and put a hand on Joshua's shoulder. They returned to the truck to get a suitcase. The sun was shinning in the blue sky above them, as it seemed to do for much of the year in the Treasure Valley.

"How was the ride. Clear flying today?"

Greg nodded. "It was kind of choppy, and the engine on the Piper is about due for an annual inspection. Going to have to take it out of action for a while."

"Well, you can still fly my Cessna whenever you want."

"Thanks Joshua, I may take you up on that. When's the last time you went up?"

Joshua looked into the bright sunlight. "Not for a while now, maybe two weeks ago? I've been busy at work lately, hard to get the time to go flying."

"Nonsense, you get a day off you go up and tool around the sky. Nothing relaxes you better than flying kid, you know that."

Greg and Joshua's father were old flying buddies. They used to go to picturesque airports all around the valley for brunches with their wives. Sheryl, Greg's wife hated to fly, but she went anyway because she loved to travel. Whenever Joshua's dad was too busy to take him flying, Joshua could always count on Greg to take him up. His own son did not like to fly, so Greg relished the chance to take Joshua up flying.

When Joshua took lessons at the Nampa airport, he often flew in Greg's Piper Cherokee. The day he was to fly solo for the first time, his father was in Japan on a business trip. Greg drove Joshua out to the airport and watched him go around the local pattern by himself. When Joshua landed he picked up his instructor and taxied back to the terminal where Greg was waiting with a long pair of scissors. It was pilot tradition to cut the shirt tail off a soloist and write the date of the event on the piece of cloth. Most instructors didn't bother with the tradition anymore but it was important to Greg. Joshua was fifteen at the time. He still had the shirt tail in a frame on the wall of his apartment.

Sheryl came out the front door and greeted Joshua with a hug. She was dressed in fleece and blue jeans, her winter flying apparel. She was an attractive woman in her early fifties with graying black hair and a dimpled smile that always made you feel welcome whenever you stopped by.

"Joshua what a surprise, it's so good to see you."

"Good to see you too."

"Did Greg tell you we just got back from Sun Valley?"

Joshua nodded as Greg retreated into the garage with another bag.

"Boy was it a bumpy ride coming home today. I had to take my Dramamine." She nudged Joshua, knowing he knew she was not thrilled with flying.

"How was the skiing?"

Sheryl's smile was big as the morning sun. "It was fantastic, fresh powder the day we got there and it snowed the whole weekend. Oh, did Greg tell you we saw Bruce Willis again? He was slumming with the locals downtown."

Sheryl loved to pretend that she was unimpressed with celebrities but Joshua knew she was a big fan of the movie actor and regularly followed up on his movies. She always watched Oprah in the afternoon and every other talk show that he was a guest on. He figured she was not alone in her fandom. Greg was aware of his wife's innocent infatuation and he liked to make fun of her for it. One time he called Joshua up to his den and showed him some official Air Force video of the big action movie star taking a flight in one of the fighter planes stationed at Mountain Home Air Force Base. The pilot took him through the rigors of faster than sound maneuvers and had the movie star ready to toss his cookies and sounding sicker than a dog.

"This is why I'm not so impressed with old Bruce. He makes it seem like he's all cool and in control in the movies but in reality the man gets sick after pulling a few g's in an F-15."

They had a good laugh after watching that video over and over again. One of Tripp's military friends had taped it on the air base's closed circuit TV channel that had it running practically nonstop.

Joshua had to smile at her mentioning of the actor. He could never watch a Bruce Willis movie again without thinking about that video.

"That's cool. Did he invite you guys over for dinner?"

Sheryl shook her head. "Oh no. We're not in his 'circle'," she said.

"So how are you doing kiddo? Tripp said you were working

on his web site again."

"I was just telling Greg we will be ready for financing in a few months."

"Great! So how is your social life? Any new girl friends?"

He knew it was only a matter of time before she got around to asking him that. She was just as nosy about his personal life as his mother had been. He didn't mind it one bit.

"Well, there is a new someone special, now that you ask," he teased.

"Do tell, do tell!"

"Her name is Dancia," he said and her mouth was open before he could get any more out.

"Isn't she on your code team?"

"Yes. We've been working pretty closely for the past few weeks. Let's just say it's looking promising."

Greg came back to the truck. "Best not to mix love and business, that's never a good thing," he interjected in his best fatherly tone.

"Don't worry dad, its cool."

Sheryl grinned broadly and patted her husband on the shoulder. "It's okay, Joshua, we'll stay out of your personal life."

Joshua remembered he was going to head over to Dancia's apartment.

"Well, I'd love to stay and chat but I've got to get going. It was nice seeing you guys again," he said, backing up for his car.

"Hey, next time stay for dinner. Maybe bring your new girlfriend?" Sheryl said with a knowing wink.

"I will. That would be fun."

"Tell our son to stop by some time, we haven't seen him in a while," Greg said. Sheryl agreed with him as they waved goodbye.

"Will do. Bye!" Joshua said, climbing back into his Porsche. He backed out into the street and waved one last time as he took off. Greg and Sheryl walked back inside the garage arm in arm. They were an awesome couple and he was lucky to have them as his surrogate family.

CHAPTER 17

JOSHUA WAS SITTING at a red light on Chinden in Garden City when he remembered the tape he had made of last night's radio chat. He looked down at his backpack and opened a side pocket, making sure it was still there. Dancia would be getting up soon. He decided to go to her place and let her translate it for him.

When he pulled up to her apartment and parked it was just after six. Trish would not be home yet but Dancia's KG was in the street. He rang the doorbell. Nothing happened. He pushed it again. Then he remembered that Dancia had disconnected it so she could sleep through the day.

He took out his cell phone and dialed her number. He heard her ring tone go off and looked around. It was coming from her car. He walked over to the Karman Ghia and looked in the passenger window. There was her cell, sitting on the passenger seat singing away.

There was no real way to get to her as they didn't have a landline. So he got back in his car and headed home. He decided he would just send her the MP3 file and she would get it when she logged on a bit later.

Joshua was hungry when he got home so he rummaged through his refrigerator until he settled on an egg sandwich. He had turned on the old radio first thing when he got home; it was warming up on the table behind him. As he waited for his eggs to cook, he put some bread in the toaster. About the time the eggs were done, the toast popped up. He squirted some ketchup on the toast and placed the egg patty between the pieces of toast.

Sitting down at the kitchen table, he opened up the laptop and started downloading the audio file from his recorder to the laptop. Then he compressed the file and emailed it to Dancia.

As he ate the egg sandwich he opened up IRC and found little to no activity. He took the sandwich and went into the living room to watch the evening news. Nix was sitting in his usual place feigning cat sleep. Joshua had fed the old cat before he started to fix his own dinner but the animal refused to make the effort to get off the couch and go eat. In his old age he only moved when he absolutely had to and then only when hunger or other urges could wait no longer.

Joshua used the remote control to go to the local news. The anchorwoman was reading from the prompter and conveying a maternal and wholesome demeanor as she read about a bribery scam. Joshua didn't normally watch local news, but when he did he usually watched the station where Tripp worked. Tripp didn't produce the nightly news only the morning news program. The weatherman came on and hinted at a big winter storm coming. As usual, no details until after the station break.

The egg sandwich did not fill him up. During the commercial break he headed back into the kitchen to get a beer and some potato chips. He checked the IRC window and saw that there was some chatting, so he picked up the laptop and took it with him back to the couch.

In the IRC chat room a new kid was trying to get the group to accept him and he was only succeeding in pissing everyone off. It was not pretty. Eventually the moderator booted the kid off. No one complained.

Joshua returned his attention to the TV and decided to change the channel. He punched in the number for a world news channel and watched that for a while. His cell phone rang.

"Hello?"

"It's me, I have a translation for you," Dancia said.

"What'd they talk about?"

There was a sigh at the other end of the phone. "Mostly poetry stuff, they talked on and on about their radios and band conditions. I tuned that crap out."

"Did they mention anything at all about music or hypnotizing people?"

"Nope. The band conditions deteriorated towards the end. I think they were talking about baseball or something about three strikes or the third strike or out three. I don't know it was pretty garbled."

Joshua remembered that band conditions were bad; he guessed that was why they signed off that night.

"I think I know how Muse got them hypnotized. He was using some kind of binaural beat music to put them into a trance. Both victims were wearing headphones so it's a possibility."

Dancia breathed heavily into the receiver for a moment.

"So maybe Muse is not a Flash programmer."

"I don't know. But I'm pretty sure he's using hypnosis and a person's fear or phobias against them. Making them think they are going to die."

Dancia yawned on her side, causing Joshua to yawn.

"Stop that."

"Sorry, I just woke up. Look, I have to get some food and wake up. Trish wants her phone back, I have no clue where my phone went off to."

"It's in your car, I stopped by earlier and tried to call you. I could hear it ringing in your car."

Dancia laughed. "What a klutz I am. It's in my car Trish! Yeah, Joshua said he rang me from the front door and he heard it going off in my car."

Joshua listened for a while as Dancia and Trish chatted.

"Hey, I'll let you two go. Talk to you later."

"Ok Joshua, bye."

He closed his phone and put it back in his front pocket. A crackle of static and someone's voice started talking on the radio in the kitchen. Joshua turned off the TV and went into the kitchen to listen.

"CQ, CQ, CQ. VE2SHM, Victor, Echo, Two, Sierra, Hotel, Mike. CQ, CQ, CQ. This is, Whiskey Five Zulu Papa Golf Charlie."

It was Muse calling Shemp. Joshua scrambled to restart his digital recorder. He managed to get it cued and recording by the time Shemp responded.

"Go head W5ZPGC, this is VE2SHM."

"Well, the conditions seem to be better this evening anyway. How's the weather up North?"

There was a pop in static and then Shemp responded. "Not too bad, clear and cold. But the weather dude on TV says we are expecting a big winter storm coming out of the West in the next few days. Is that going to hit you at all? Over."

Their voices sounded like heavy Cylons from the original *Battlestar Galactica* TV series. Joshua reminded himself that they were probably running voice-altering software filters to further mask their identities. He found it odd that they had not switched to French yet.

"I think we are expecting some snow at the higher elevations. We usually get a few flurries around here, but nothing lasts more than a few days. Good for the local ski lodges though. Over."

They went on like that, talking about nothing in particular. Joshua started to get bored. He was hoping one of them would let something interesting slip out. But they kept up the idle prattle for a good hour. The band was holding and their signals were both coming in pretty clear. Muse was talking about living in Florida as a kid.

"We used to skim over the marsh in those things like bats out of hell. Those were the good old days. One time we saw them launch a rocket from out on the swamp. It was far out, man. It lit up the whole damn area right at sunset."

Joshua sat up. *Far out? Who the hell says that any more?* Then it hit him. *Taggert said that just today.* Joshua's heart started to race and he broke out in a sudden sweat. *Lawrence Taggert was Muse! He had to be! Didn't he say something about coming to Boise with Joshua's father from Florida?* Joshua knew that his parents had grown up in Florida and that his dad had worked for NASA there. "Holy shit, Muse knows me!"

Suddenly Joshua was too scared to even move. He stared at the twin dials of the radio and tried to think what Glenn had done to possibly offend Taggert. The two men continued to talk on the radio, but Joshua's mind was racing. *Does Taggert know that I'm on to him? How could he? He never mentioned anything to anyone about what he was doing. Except for Nik! Did Nik say anything to Taggert? No way, the two of them never spoke before. Why would they talk now?* Joshua wiped his brow and tried to calm himself down.

Maybe he doesn't know. He can't know. Why would he suspect that I was looking for him? He can't know, damn it. He can't know. Joshua took a few deep breaths.

"I'm striking again. That kid from the channel," Muse said coldly on the radio.

"Why? Do you think it's him?" Shemp asked.

Joshua's eyes froze as he stared in horror at the little brown radio.

"Yes, I'll let you know how it goes. Well, I better get some things ready. Nice chatting with you. Stay warm. We'll talk again soon. W5ZPGC clear."

"Ok, take it easy. This is VE2SHM."

The band returned to the normal low levels of static and popping noises. Muse was going to kill someone again, someone from the IRC chat room. *He was going to kill Nooblet.* Joshua jumped up out of his seat and fished out his cell phone. He dialed Dancia's number as fast as he could.

The phone rang, and rang and rang. *Damn, she left it in the car!* Joshua didn't know Stacy's number. He had to warn Dancia somehow. He ran into the living room and scooped up his laptop. She was not in the chat room. He quickly emailed her and told her to get off her computer and call him. *What if she were out? What if she were already being attacked? What if I am too late?*

Joshua ran for the door.

CHAPTER 18

THE MUSIC WAS a smooth and relaxing Jazz Fusion. Dancia preferred classic Jazz like Coltrane or Mingus, but sometimes the new Fusion hit the spot for her. She pressed the padded earphones to her head and sat back in her computer chair. She could easily fall asleep again listening to this music.

She opened her eyes and stared at the computer screen. She was watching the Visualizer that came with iTunes on full screen. It displayed a swirling, trail of light and color that moved with the beat of the music. Dancia had seen someone on #own3d chatting about a cool new Jazz feed he had found before she came home in the morning. She had to see what it was like. Her head was bouncing ever so slightly to the unusual beat.

She did not notice that several of her running programs had shut down. The only programs left running were X-Chat Aqua and iTunes. Everything else was shut down seconds after the buffer overflow. The hiccup that iTunes made just as it hooked up to the feed, was her program dying and a new one starting. One that was under the control of Muse.

A buffer overflow was about the only way for a bad guy to break into a UNIX system. It was caused when a program was flooded with extraneous data into its memory buffers. Muse had discovered a way to break iTunes with a buffer overflow that was caused by a reference to memory that did not exist. It was a pointer in the code that referred to a null value. The exploit was unknown to anyone but him and when used allowed him to gain access to her computer.

He could not take complete control of her computer, as he was only able to access programs under her user name. That was all he needed to be able to shut her off from the outside world by turning off her Mail program and making sure system sounds never reached her earphones.

The version of iTunes she was now listening to was a special version that ran code supplied by Muse. The music and images she was seeing began to lull her into an altered state of consciousness. After a few minutes of the binaural beat infused music she was completely under his control.

/*--*/

The heat was oppressive. Even the warm water from her water bottle felt good sliding down her parched throat. Beck, her driver with the tinted goggles kept looking at her. She sighed as more of the breeze blew at her face like a hair dryer.

"I don't like this, man, got a bad feeling," Beck said, looking around at the deserted section of Bagdad they were moving through.

"Come on Beck, you're scaring me. We'll be fine. Only a few more klics to go."

He nodded, but the uneasy look on his face reflected his concern. She gripped the M-16 in her lap and put her finger on the safety. Just in case.

An explosion ripped through the lead HUMVEE in the convoy. Parts of it impacted the glass on their one-ton's window two vehicles behind the lead. Dancia screamed and Beck tried to swerve around the wreckage following the truck in front of them.

"Son of a bitch! I knew we'd get hit," Beck yelled as they kept going past the smoke.

Dancia could see figures moving in front of them. She heard the popping sounds of AK-47 rounds going off. Several rounds struck their truck. She pointed her rifle out her window and fired. Anything that moved was shot.

The one-ton truck rocked with an explosion and she was thrust forward into the dashboard. The butt of her M-16 smashed her forehead. Her left wrist broke against the dash. In a slow moving blur, she could hear her wrist snap and feel the sudden pain. She was not wearing a seatbelt and came to rest on the floor of the cab.

Looking up she saw Beck hit several times with small arms fire and slump over at the wheel. The big tan truck lurched forward into the truck in front of them and then stopped as his foot fell off the clutch. There was another violent explosion and a grinding sound as the truck behind them plowed into their rear.

More shots could be heard as the platoon was returning fire. Dancia looked up at Beck. His eyes were open, but he was dead. Pools of blood were forming in his flack jacket and spilling out onto the floor of the one-ton.

She was too terrified to even move. She flinched at every shot fired. Pop, pop-pop-pop. Her heart raced with the automatic gunfire. Her wrist throbbed with pain so badly that she wanted to pass out. The thought occurred to her that she would die here. She didn't want to die.

She reloaded the M-16 with her one good hand. It was not easy but she managed. She could hear men shouting in Arabic. They were getting closer. More machine gun fire, louder this time. It was a fifty-caliber gun. Hope welled up inside her for the first time. She loved the thundering sound of that big gun.

A bearded face appeared above her. It was an insurgent. His dark eyes grew large when he saw her. He started to holler at her. She shot him between the eyes. There was silence until his lifeless form hit the ground. The side of the truck erupted in exploding bullets.

```
/*-------------------------------------------------*/
```

It took Joshua nearly fifteen minutes to get the few blocks down

the street to Dancia's. There was a traffic incident that blocked
Front Street.

The wait seemed like an eternity to him. At one point he
even contemplated ditching the Porsche and running. After
finally being let through he gunned the little sports car, breaking
all speed limits until he skidded to a halt before her house.

Stacey's car was gone. The front door would be locked. He
would have to bust it down or find another way in. Bounding
from the car he bolted up to the front porch and tried the door.
It was locked. He pound hard on the door then he moved to the
front window and tried to look inside. There were no lights on
inside. Maybe she had stepped out and was not home.

Bolting up the front porch, he tried the door. Locked like he
thought. He pounded on the door, then the window frame as he
tried to look in. Maybe she had stepped out and was not home.

But he knew better.

His heart raced. "Dancia! Dancia!" he yelled as he pounded
on the door.

Still pounding, then kicking with his foot, he flipped the
doormat up. Nothing.

His eyes flashed to the lock. *Flimsy. No double lock. I can
do this.*

He put is foot into it like in the movies. Nothing. Barely a
budge. Stepping back, Joshua could feel the panic rising. His
heart beat so hard, it was going to jump out of his chest. He
breathed in gasps.

I'am going to be too late!

"NO!" He rammed his shoulder into the door.

He stumbled into the room as the door burst inward. Ruined.
Not that he cared, or even felt the pain in his shoulder.

"Dancia!"

/*---*/

The hail of bullets ripped into the passenger side of the one-ton.

Her leg caught one bullet grazing her calf. She felt the sting like a snake had bitten her. Most of the rounds went into Beck's corpse and the ceiling above the driver side. She did not return fire. Hoping that they wrote her off and would move on. The screaming and confusion outside only intensified.

She considered crawling out the driver's door but she knew they would gun her down before she managed to find cover. More gunfire was directed at her truck. This time the engine caught on fire and started to burn. Either she got out and took her chances or she would burn up in the truck. Her wrist hurt so bad she could barely think straight. She slid up on the front seat and peered out the bullet holes in the side door. She didn't see any movement. The fighting sounded like it had moved on to the rear of the convoy.

She opened the door and pointed the M-16 outside. Flames were rising fast from the engine and the bulkhead was beginning to feel warm. She had to get out before the fuel tanks exploded. It was a long way down to the ground. She hesitated just long enough for a Marine to appear through the smoke and grab her from the truck. She fell on him as they both hit the ground.

"Thanks," she said. Then she realized that he was not moving. She looked up in time to see three insurgent gunmen racking the charging handles of their Kalashnikov riffles.

Dancia's heart stopped. She was about to die. She heard a voice calling her name over and over again. The voice got louder and louder until she could no longer hear the burning truck or the popping sounds of machine gun fire. The repressive desert heat and the smell of cordite faded away.

She opened her eyes and a man's face slowly came into focus above her. It was Joshua. He had awakened her from the nightmare.

Dancia was wet with perspiration and trembling with fear as she sat up in her chair. She held onto Joshua with a tight grip.

"Dancia, it's okay. You're safe now," Joshua said. He

brought her head to his chest in a hug.

Seeing her seemingly asleep at her computer with the padded headphones on, fueled his anger and sent him over the edge. He could not bear to loose her, she was too important to him. Joshua realized in that harrowing instant that he was in love with her. No matter how hard he had denied himself the possibility, he was now fully committed to her in heart and soul.

"I was in Iraq. They were ready to kill me. It was so," she paused. Her heart was still pumped up on adrenaline, causing her to tremble. "Real. I thought I was going to die."

"You were under hypnosis and Muse was using your memories of the war to try and frighten you into thinking you were going to die. It's how he killed Zemo and Glenn. I got here as fast as I could."

She pushed away from him for the first time. He looked down into her deep brown eyes and saw the anger in them. "How did he do that to me? How could he get to me?" she asked.

They both looked back at her monitor. The screen was black.

"I was listening to a music stream on iTunes."

Joshua bumped the mouse and hit the Escape key. The music program returned to normal mode. He opened a terminal window and checked what processes were running. Only iTunes and the IRC chat program were running. He looked closer. There were two instances of iTunes open. One process was hung the other running.

"I have no idea."

She nudged him away from the keyboard. "Do you think he's still on now?"

"Maybe, I don't see how he could know if you were still alive or dead. He must have come through the stream kind of like what he did on Glenn's box to get to him at work."

She looked at him and nodded in agreement.

"I know who Muse is. It's a guy I work with named Lawrence Taggert."

She blinked. "Do you think he thought I was you?"

"No, I'm betting he wants us both dead."

Dancia checked for open ports. There was a secure shell connection to an open port. She opened a terminal and used it to send a system message to everyone connected to her computer.

Broadcast Message from dancia@dancias-computer.local (/dev/ttyp2) at 8:52 MDT... You lose, FUCKER! I know who you are.

Joshua grinned. Dancia looked pleased with herself. "Let's make him sweat for a change."

She ran another command called "*who -Hmu*" that showed her who was connected to the computer. There was only one connection, herself.

"We have to go to the police with this," Joshua said.

Dancia nodded solemnly. She looked at him seriously. "Thank you for saving me."

He put his hands on the back of her head and brought her close to him. Her wrist felt sore as she put her arms around him. But she didn't care. She pressed against him hard and they kissed passionately, as if they might never kiss again.

CHAPTER 19

BEFORE THEY LEFT for the police station, Joshua found some nails and a hammer and did his best to repair the front door frame. It would not be as strong as it had been for him, but it would at least keep the door shut. They left a note for Stacey telling her what happened, since she was out on a date.

Joshua told Dancia to get some clothes and other things together before they left. They would be going out of town for a while. She found her book bag from school and filled it with underwear, jeans and a few different shirts. Then she raided her bathroom and took a few personal necessities. When she was ready, Joshua was finishing up with the front door.

"Where are we going to go?" she asked him.

"McCall, I own a family cabin up there. We can stay there as long as it takes the police to capture Muse and Shemp. No sense making it easy for them to find us."

McCall Idaho was a small lakeside resort community a few hours north of Boise. Nearly everyone in Boise seemed to have a cabin there. Dancia was surprised that Joshua had never mentioned it to her before. She figured it was probably not the only thing she didn't know about him.

They got into Joshua's Porsche and went straight to the Boise Police station. The detective assigned to their case was not on duty and they had to wait for him to be called in. The station was nearly empty at ten on a Wednesday night. They talked about who Muse was and how Joshua figured out who he was. Everything seemed to make sense to them, whether they could convince the detective was yet to be seen.

Detective Bill Plait was used to being called in on a weeknight. It happened so frequently that he no longer jumped when his beeper went off at night. He called the station to get the details of the case as he drove in.

It sounded like a couple of scared kids who thought someone was trying to kill them over their computers. That was a new one.

He went straight for the coffee machine when he got in, filled up his mug and headed into the holding area where Joshua and Dancia were sitting. They certainly looked like normal kids. Both were dressed in simple jeans and T-shirts with winter coats lying on the bench beside them. The girl was wearing dark rimmed glasses and the boy looked to be slightly older but with a youthful face.

"Hello folks, I'm detective Bill Plait," he said.

"Detective, I'm Joshua Jones and this is Dancia Rivers," Joshua said, standing up and offering his hand.

Detective Plait shook Joshua's hand. "I understand you kids had a scary incident on your computer?"

Joshua and Dancia looked at each other. "You could say that," Joshua said.

They moved into a briefing room away from the lobby. Plait offered them some coffee and they both took him up on it. When they were comfortable, Joshua began by telling him about the death of his coworker out at RegTech. The detective's expression remained indifferent as he listened to Joshua. He started taking notes on a yellow legal pad as Joshua began to explain the technical bits about computer security and how Muse was able to break into both victims' computers.

Plait was not a computer geek, but he did know a few things about how they worked and to the best of his knowledge what Joshua was saying rang true to him. He was impressed by how detailed their efforts to find Muse were. They didn't actually break any laws in what they did, but they probably should have come in to talk sooner.

Detective Plait jotted down some more notes after Joshua finished talking. "If what you've told me can be corroborated by our tech guys, this Taggert sounds pretty dangerous. However, we don't really have any direct evidence that this Muse character is Taggert. He never said on the radio who he was going to attack and he never admitted that he had killed anyone else."

"But who else could it be?" Joshua interrupted.

Plait sat back and looked at both of them. He could tell they were upset and their emotions were probably running high.

"Look, the best we can do is find this Taggert fellow and bring him in for questioning. Maybe I can get a warrant to search his house, but unless we find something incriminating we just won't be able to press charges."

Joshua looked disappointed. "He knows we know who he is. He knows we figured out how he's done it. Don't you think he might just come after me now?"

Plait could see the fear in the young kid's eyes, but there really wasn't anything they could do for him. "If you are concerned for your safety I suggest you not go home tonight. Check into a hotel and let us have some time to bring him in for questioning. If he's guilty, he may try and run. But if he can't find you, he can't get to you."

Dancia tossed up her hands in defeat. "Look, this asshole tried to kill me tonight! We're both in danger here."

"I understand that Miss Rivers. All I am saying is that my hands are tied until I get a search warrant."

Joshua shook his head. "Okay, I understand. But we're not sticking around. I'll leave you our cell numbers and the address where we will be for the rest of the week. If you find out anything, give us a call."

"Where will you be staying?"

"McCall, I have a cabin there," Joshua said.

"You realize that McCall is out of our jurisdiction? I can't protect you up there, the best I can do is make the McCall police aware of your situation."

"I understand. Tonight we'll stay with a friend of mine and we will head North in the morning. What are you going to do about the guy in Canada?"

"I'll get in touch with the authorities in his home town and they will deal with it as they see fit. We have good relations with our Northern neighbors so if he's guilty of corroboration, it should be easy enough to haul him in."

"What about the radio violations? Muse is using bogus amateur radio call signs. The least you that you could do would be to notify the FCC about him."

Plait put down his pen and smiled. "You're right. I'll start the ball rolling on that issue too. Look, you kids just need to calm down and let me do my job. Things will work themselves out, they always do."

When they left the police station Joshua called Steve and asked him if they could crash at his place for the night. Steve agreed without hesitation. They arrived at Steve's place shortly before midnight. He was rolling out some sleeping bags for them in his TV room.

"We've got to stop meeting like this, you guys," Steve said as he let them inside.

Dancia gave him a weak smile as she headed for his bathroom. Joshua shook Steve's hand and thanked him again, and then he motioned for them to go into Steve's radio shack.

Inside the shack Joshua whispered. "I need to borrow a hand

gun for a few days."

Steve's face came alive. He loved guns. "Personal defense?"

Joshua nodded grimly. Steve put his hand on Joshua's back and led him over to his gun safe. He unlocked the cabinet and took out several handguns and set them on the work bench.

There was a small caliber PPK, a Colt Model 1911 and a large revolver that Joshua figured was a 357 Magnum.

"Take your pick my friend. But if you ask me, I'd use the Colt."

Joshua knew very little about guns. He just wanted something that was easy to shoot and reliable. He picked up the Colt and held it in his hand to feel it's weight. It was solid and cold but it felt right in his large hand.

He raised it up. "This will do, I'm sure."

"How much ammo you think you'll need?" Steve asked as he put the other guns back in the cabinet.

"I don't know. How many rounds are in the clip?"

"Seven. You better take a box, you can pay me back later," Steve said, handing him a box of forty-five caliber bullets.

If he could help it, Joshua wouldn't be firing any shots at all. He was just being cautious. Dancia came into the room and saw him holding the Colt. She came over and looked at Joshua.

"Do you think you'll need that?"

"The cabin is kind of remote up there, it would be prudent to be prepared."

She agreed. He handed her the large handgun. She was trained on the Beretta nine-millimeter handgun in the Marines. The Italian gun was sleeker and more elegant, but the Colt was undeniably more powerful and masculine. She imagined pointing it at Muse and pulling the trigger. Nothing would give her more pleasure after what he tried tonight. She handed the gun back to Joshua and headed towards the TV room.

"Muse tried to kill her tonight. We're heading out of town for a few days to give the police time to bring him in."

Steve looked at him suspiciously. "Have you ever fired a pistol before?"

"No."

Steve launched into his gun safety speech and Joshua listened intently. He watched as Steve broke the gun down, removed the magazine, showed him the safety, how to move the slide. He let Joshua mess with the empty gun for a while in order to get a feel for it. Convinced that his friend could handle the weapon, he set out looking for a holster. He found one under the workbench and handed it to Joshua.

"Who did it turn out to be, anyway?" Steve asked.

"Lawrence Taggert, a guy I work with."

Steve thought for a moment. "Taggert sounds familiar. He may be in my Ham club. Wait, I think I have heard of him."

Steve moved back to his radio table and pulled out a logbook and started flipping through the spiral bound pages. "What does he look like?"

"He's about my height, thinning brown hair, grayish eyes. Always wears jeans and cowboy boots and a big leather belt, not very talkative, at least at work. He's chatty on the radio."

Steve smiled. "Ham geeks are like that. Timid and shy in real life, but get them on the radio and suddenly they have a personality. I guess I haven't worked him lately. Are the police going to turn him in to the FCC?"

"The detective said he would handle it. Not sure if that will be a priority for him but if it gets Taggert off the streets, all the better."

Steve put the logbook down and they moved back into the TV room. Dancia had claimed the couch and was already lying down, watching the news.

"Thanks for letting us crash Steve. We'll be out of here early in the morning."

"No problem. Where are you guys heading anyway?" Steve asked.

"I don't know, one of the resorts maybe?" He didn't want to tell anyone any more than he had to.

Steve agreed it was a good idea to lay low for a while. He left them alone and retired to his bedroom down the hall. Joshua sat down in the big easy chair and put up the footrest. The weather was on and it looked like a big winter storm was brewing in Oregon.

"We'll head out of here early in the morning. I think we'll fly up. I don't want to have him follow us by car. I'll get Steve to drop us off at the Nampa airport."

Dancia looked at him. "You mean in your little puddle jumper?"

"Don't worry. We'll be fine. You'll see."

CHAPTER 20

IT WAS STILL dark out when Steve dropped them off at the hangar where Joshua kept his airplane. The stars were shinning in the sky. Dancia had put the handgun in her backpack so it was out of sight. She had the backpack hanging off her shoulder as she waited for Joshua to unlock the main hangar door.

Standing in the bitter cold she was already missing the warmth of Steve's car. It was a long drive out to Nampa and the car had become real toasty. They stopped for breakfast at a drive-through McDonald's just off the interstate. She was still finishing her coffee.

Joshua pulled open the lock and then started to slide the metal hangar doors open. Dancia pushed on one and it seemed to travel easier than the side that Joshua was pushing. Once the doors were open Dancia opened the passenger door of the shiny metal airplane and tossed in her backpack. She looked at how tiny the cockpit was and remembered that she really didn't like flying in small planes.

Joshua untied the ropes that anchored the plane to the concrete floor of the hangar, letting them fall back towards the rear of the hangar so that they would not become entangled in the plane's propeller. He started going over the pre-flight checklist in his head as he moved around the plane. He checked the tires and brakes, ran his hands over the trailing edge of the wing, testing the control surfaces. Then followed the leading edge back to the nose where the engine compartment was. He unlocked the lunch box latches and opened the cowling to check the oil level, holding a small Mag light to see what he was doing. He stuck his hand in the inlets, looking for bird's nests or spider webs. Then he ran a hand over the single propeller blade, feeling for nicks or other imperfections. The plane was inside the hangar and probably didn't need such a thorough looking over, but he did it anyway out of habit.

He got a thin plastic beaker out of the plane and used it to drain fuel out of the wing tanks to look for water. If there were water in the tanks it would show up at the drain points. The light blue tinted aviation gas in both tanks was not tainted with water. He moved down the fuselage checking for missing rivets, broken linkage and anything not where it should be. He moved the metal control surfaces of the horizontal stabilizer and checked the hinges on the curvy rudder.

Joshua's grandfather had purchased the plane direct from the factory in Wichita Kansas back in 1946. He had been a fighter pilot in the Second World War and he used the little metal plane to run a flight school in McCall back in the early fifties. Joshua had every annual and maintenance record the plane had ever endured for its entire life. Some time in the mid-sixties his grandfather had it upgraded to a beefier electrical system and metal covered control surfaces. In the late seventies, he sold it to Joshua's father to keep the plane in the family. Joshua's father invested in a complete restoration in the mid-eighties and ever since Joshua had owned the plane he maintained it as carefully as he did his Porsche.

It was a classic two-seat airplane with rounded wings and tail and a shiny metal surface set off by a sky blue stripe that came off the nose and tapered to a point about half way to the tail on both sides. Joshua's first trip in an airplane was in the friendly old bird. His grandfather had taken him for a ride when he was four and he promptly fell asleep. He was back on the ground before he woke up, thanks to his grandfather's light touch on landings. It was the first of many flights and the birth of the aviation bug in Joshua's heart.

Joshua let Dancia climb in to the cabin on the starboard side so she would at least be out of the cold. When he finished his pre-flight walk around, he pushed the plane out of the hangar and stopped it just clear of the doors. Then he slid the metal doors shut and locked them.

Inside the cramped cockpit he blew some hot air onto his hands to warm them up.

"I'll have the heat on in a moment."

He got out a check sheet and started moving controls and tapping instrument dials in preparation for cranking the engine. Finally, he opened the window and hollered outside. "Clear!"

The engine roared to life with little coercion from him. He let it idle for a few minutes as he put on his headset and adjusted the radios. There was a second headset that he urged Dancia to put on. Engine noise was such that if you wanted to actually talk with your passenger, you both had to wear headsets and use an intercom.

Eventually, he let go of the foot brakes and the Cessna 120 started moving down the taxi strip heading for the main runway. He clicked the microphone on the tower frequency to bring up the runway lights.

Dancia liked the colored lights; they distracted her from thinking about how small the plane was. At the end of the active runway, Joshua did an engine run-up to make sure it was working correctly and then throttled down. He made a sweep of the sky around the airport, looking for any traffic in the pattern. Seeing none, he pulled out onto the active after alerting the airport on the radio.

"Cessna two five two whiskey mike, departing Nampa Municipal on two-niner."

No one responded because the tower was unmanned. He

edged the little plane out on the active and pushed the throttle forward all the way. Gently letting off the brakes, the airplane roared down the runway. Dancia felt her heart race as they gained speed. They were not really going any faster than a car on the interstate.

The tail of the Cessna rose up first, and Joshua kept the plane level with a slight upward tilt as it gained enough speed for take off. Then he gently pulled back the control yoke and they left the surly bonds of Earth and soared into the clear morning sky.

In minutes they had climbed above the city of Nampa and were heading north by northwest towards the mountains. Joshua had made this trip so many times and in so many different weather conditions, he really didn't have to think much about where he was going. There were familiar landmarks and little mining towns along the way, but mostly he followed Highway 55 which in turn followed the Payette River that wound its way through the mountains and high plateaus all the way to McCall.

At one point along the river he pointed down to a bend in the road beside the river and said. "That's where my parents died." He didn't have to say any more, Dancia knew the story. One night a few months back they were hacking on Tripp's movie database and he had told her about the death of his parents. How the family car had slipped off the icy road and fell upside down into the freezing river. How the police had determined that his parents became trapped inside the car even as he had managed to escape and they had drowned in the cold water of the river. It was a freak accident that claimed their lives as well as countless other lives over the years. Winter driving was not to be taken lightly by Joshua again. It was many years before he could drive to McCall by himself during the winter months. He usually flew there, as if soaring above the accident site protected him from seeing that bend in the road.

Dancia looked down at the white landscape and marveled at how pristine it all looked from the air. How untouched by the hand of man. She understood a little better now why he loved to fly. It kind of separated you from the immediacy of your day-to-day grind. It put some distance from the petty little concerns of everyday life and let you see the greater scheme of life that you were a part of.

They arrived over McCall about thirty minutes later. Stiff head winds had slowed their progress, but had not rocked them hard enough to make them feel uneasy. They circled over the lakeside resort town once, so that Joshua could enter the airport flight pattern from near the center of town. Joshua touched down with as much skill and grace as his grandfather had. They weaved their way back to the main row of airplanes and parked in front of another metal hangar.

It was much colder in McCall and there were snowdrifts all around. The concrete entrance to Joshua's hangar had been plowed; the older, icy snow was still in piles at ether side of the hangar doors. He took out his keys and opened the lock. The metal doors slid much easier and he opened one side all the way. Inside was an old Jeep Wrangler with a hard top. He climbed inside and started it up, cranking the heater for Dancia.

He drove it out past the airplane and parked it. He moved open the left hangar door and together the two of them pushed and pulled the Cessna 120 into the hangar backwards. There was a winter storm coming in the next few days, and he wanted the antique airplane out of the elements.

Dancia got into the Jeep with her backpack and waited for him to tie down the airplane and secure the hangar. When he climbed into the driver's seat, the Jeep was warmed up.

"Ok, let's go," he said with a smile. She nodded. It really had been a pleasant trip and she was thankful he had insisted they fly.

They drove through McCall and commented on how dead it was for the season. The locals were battening down the hatches and getting ready for the next winter storm. Joshua pulled the

Jeep into the parking lot of the largest grocery store in town and they went inside to buy some perishables. He kept the cabin well stocked with canned goods but if they wanted fresh milk and vegetables they had to get them now.

The family cabin was nestled into a bend beside the Payette River not far from the airport. It was an A-frame cabin with two stories and was painted dark brown. The nearest cabin was a hundred feet away but there was no one home. The owners wintered in Arizona and only spent the summer months in McCall. There was still about six inches of snow around the property from the last storm, but it had melted off the porch.

Dancia got out of the Jeep and stood on solid ground. She looked up at the cabin and smiled. There was a simple, rustic charm to the place that she instantly liked. Joshua stepped up to the front door and unlocked it. Just inside the foyer was a snow room, a place to take off your boots and change out of your winter garb. There were fishing poles in a corner and floppy fishing hats on the coat rack. An old set of wooden skies was mounted on the wall. They had belonged to Joshua's grandfather back in the 50's when the cabin was first built.

"Go ahead and look around, I'll bring in the groceries," Joshua said, heading back out to the Jeep.

Dancia walked down the hall that led to the back of the cabin. There was a small bathroom and a bedroom complete with a queen sized bed and dressers. Everything looked like it had been there for ages and held hundreds of stories of family summers and winters spent there over the years. There were a bunch of framed family pictures on the wall, a monument to the cabin's owners and the good times had by all over the years.

The kitchen was fully loaded with modern, burnt orange appliances from the 1970's. There was a dining table and a open family room that housed a circular fireplace against the far wall.

A staircase angled around and went upstairs to more bedrooms and a second bathroom. Dancia walked to the back of the main room and looked out the sliding glass door to the wooden deck outside. You could see the river just beyond a shallow backyard.

Joshua came in and set the groceries down on the island that separated the kitchen area from the family room. He started putting away the refrigerated items. Dancia came over to help and learned where he kept things like glasses, dishes and silverware.

They decided to make a pot of spaghetti for dinner and for lunch they would go out to My Father's Place, a local burger joint that served huge traditional burgers and really tasty fries. Joshua figured he had enough food and DVDs to keep them entertained for the rest of the week. They hoped the police would be able to bring in Taggert by then.

CHAPTER 21

DETECTIVE BILL PLAIT was in early for a Wednesday morning. He wanted to make sure the ball got rolling on the search warrant for Lawrence Taggert and that the Canadian police were alerted so that they could try and find Mike Metz. It was always interesting dealing with the Canadian authorities; they seemed to have many different law enforcement divisions and most of them overlapped in some areas. He was able to reach the *Sûreté du Québec* and they were going to send a patrol car out to the kid's residence to see if they could speak with him.

He also had to contact the "C" Division of the RCMP (Royal Canadian Mounted Police) due to the fact that this could turn into an international investigation, which meant that he would have to bring in the FBI. Something told him that it was going to be a long day. The last thing he wanted was to involve all those agencies and then have it turn out to be nothing, or a prank of some sort. Plait had a pretty good feel for people and he was confident that the kids were not pranking him last night.

Around ten that morning he got his search warrant to check out Taggert's home. He took a squad car with him for back up and another detective. They drove out to the northern edge of Ada County to Taggert's trailer. It was parked on top of a ridge that was part of the Boise Foothills. You couldn't miss the forty-foot radio antenna that hung above the property. There was only one road up the side of the hill to the house and it looked like a pretty steep drop off to the far side of the ridge. The DMV had a late model Dodge Ram truck registered to Taggert but there were no vehicles to be found anywhere.

He thought about sending one of the troopers around back, in case Taggert made a dash for it on foot. The rough terrain made that a poor exit route, so he dropped the idea. They stood away from the front door with their weapons drawn, better to error on the side of caution. Everyone was wearing body armor but that didn't always work with a large caliber rifle.

Plait pounded on the door and rang the doorbell. He was required to identify himself and his intentions before entry and he did so with authority. There was no response. The house was quiet.

He motioned for one of the troopers to open the door. It was not locked. Sensing a trap, he followed the trooper with a shotgun into the house. It was empty. They moved with caution around the various rooms and reconvened in the front living room. It may have been empty, but there were signs that someone had been home recently.

There was some camping gear strewn around on the floor and a couple of empty boxes of nine millimeter ammunition in the waste basket, but by and large the place looked normal. Plait and the other detective set about looking for anything that could link Taggert to what the kids had accused him of.

Plait had seen a computer room back down the main hall, so he started there. There was only one computer in the room. It was housed in a large server box with caster wheels on the bottom that looked like a doghouse to Plait. The monitor was on, but there was only a command line interface with a silent, blinking curser.

His eyes scanned the desk and bookshelves, mostly old UNIX manuals and some very old hardware that probably no longer functioned. It was clear the guy was an old school geek. There were a few Ham radios on the desk, again, older type gear that judging from the amount of chrome trim was new back in the seventies. None of the radio equipment was on.

Plait found a paper logbook on the desk and read some of the contacts made in pencil. It was all pretty esoteric and near as he could tell, normal. None of the latest contacts were from Canada. But that would be expected if he were covering his bases.

There were lots of wires coming out of the radio gear and going into what looked like a speaker box and an antenna-switching box. More wires went from the back of the radios to the back of the computer. The kid, Joshua, had noted in his report that he thought Muse was using voice altering software to disguise himself on the air. That would appear to be correct from what Plait could tell. He was no engineer.

The detective called for him and Plait left the room for the back yard. They had found a makeshift shooting range in the back yard. There were shell casings lying around in the dirt and snow. Plait bent down and picked one up to smell it. The brass was cold and smelled of sulfur.

It looked like Taggert was getting in a little target practice this morning. Plait studied the radio antenna while he was outside. It was made from triangular tubing and braced with four guy wires that were mounted on eyelets that were cemented into the ground. The wind was blowing pretty steady up on the hilltop and Plait guessed that during a storm the winds were quite a bit stronger.

He turned the brass over in his hand and thought about the other case he was working. A nine-millimeter bullet killed Henry Levine. He was also a Ham. Plait went back inside the computer room and looked around. There was some equipment stacked in a corner that looked like it was radio related. He picked up a metal cover that had been removed from one of the electronic boxes between the computer and the radios. Turning it over he saw Henry Levine's call sign written inside. At that moment Taggert went from a person of interest to a suspect.

Plait took out his cell phone again and called the McCall police station. He knew the police chief there and was put through to him immediately.

"Pete, this is Bill. Yeah, doing fine, yourself?" He listened politely for a moment as Pete went on about how nice and quiet it was for early in the season.

"That's great, listen I need you to send a car out to a cabin up there for me. Just check in on some kids and make sure they are okay." Plait gave his friend the address to Joshua's cabin and then hung up. He took out his notebook and a pen, and started making notes about what he found.

There was no evidence that linked Taggert to McCall. So it was a good bet that they would be safe, but he didn't want to chance it. He radioed into dispatch to put out an APB for Taggert's Dodge truck and a warrant for his arrest. With any luck they would find him at a local area store and bring him in.

His cell went off. "Detective Plait."

It was the Quebec Police. Mike Metz was found dead in his apartment at his computer with no evidence of foul play. They were moving the case to homicide and the RCMP was coming in to take it over.

At his computer? Plait quickly asked if Metz was wearing head phones - he was. Plait looked around the room with renewed interest. The style of killing sounded too similar to be a coincidence.

Plait spent a good twenty minutes talking to several detectives on the Canadian side, answering all their questions to the best of his ability. His next call was to the Salt Lake City Division of the FBI. He spent another thirty minutes talking with the Special Agents assigned to both computer crimes and violent crimes divisions. When everyone had been briefed he was told by the FBI to stay at the house and that they were sending an Agent out there immediately.

It was starting to cloud up towards the West and obvious that a major snowstorm was brewing. Plait continued to look around the property, hoping to find some bit of evidence that would definitely link Taggert to Joshua Jones. It was almost noon when he called Joshua's cell number.

"Hello?"

"Joshua Jones?" Plait asked.

"Speaking."

"This is Detective Plait, Boise Police Department."

"Yes sir," Joshua replied, wiping his mouth and sitting up in the booth. He and Dancia were just finishing their burgers for lunch.

"I just got word from Canada that Mike Metz was found dead in his apartment. This is rapidly turning into a serious situation."

Joshua blinked and stared in disbelief at Dancia. She gave him a curious look, wondering who was on the phone.

"Shemp is dead?" Joshua repeated. Dancia's eyes grew big.

"Yes. In a few minutes the FBI will be taking over this case. I've already briefed them about the situation. They want you to stay put for the time being. I've spoken to the police chief up there in McCall and he's agreed to send a car by your place to check on you."

Joshua nodded, as if he were listening to the detective in person.

"You still there, kid?"

"Yes sir."

"Good, we have an APB out on Taggert, he's wanted in connection with another murder. We should have him located in short order. Until then, stay where you are."

Joshua thanked the detective and then hung up. Dancia had held herself in check, but he could tell she was shocked that Shemp was dead. Joshua moved to her side of the booth and hugged her. She appreciated the support and clung to him tightly. Snow was beginning to fall in huge, gentle flakes.

"I felt like I knew him and now he's dead," she said.

Joshua squeezed her shoulder.

"I know. There's been far too much death in our lives lately. But don't worry, the cops will find Taggert and everything will be fine."

"They always are," she said sarcastically.

They sat there quietly for a moment, as if out of respect for Shemp. Joshua elected not to tell her that Taggert was wanted for another murder back in Boise.

CHAPTER 22

DANCIA PLOPPED DOWN on the couch and watched the snowfall outside the picture windows. The sky was gray behind the tall pine trees that flanked the river. She loved to watch the snow falling. It relaxed her. Joshua started getting the ingredients for spaghetti ready to cook. He found a nice yellow onion and put it on a cutting board. Then he took a chef's knife out of a drawer and began sliding it up and down a sharpening steel. It was a rhythmic motion that his father had taught him long ago. After a few minutes of sharpening he cut into the onion and soon had it diced and ready to toss into the skillet.

His family's recipe for spaghetti was simple but very delicious. It took him only a few minutes to sauté the onions and brown the ground beef. As he added ingredients and stirred them, he thought about Shemp and how he had been killed. It was ironic that the man who had professed to having hypnotized someone was killed by the very same method. Taggert had very cleverly killed two others at their computers and would likely have gotten away with it had he not left calling cards in their code. Joshua wondered if by doing that, Taggert was trying to be found. Perhaps he wanted someone to eventually figure out how the killings were done and by whom. As he set the sauce to simmer he couldn't help but think that Taggert had been trying all along to get Joshua to solve the murder.

Again, it was the motive that haunted him now about the

situation. *What had he ever done to Taggert to warrant that kind of hatred?* Joshua had no idea. He moved to the great room and sat down on the couch beside Dancia. Her face was sullen and her eyes heavy behind her glasses.

She looked around the inside of the cabin for the first time. Sitting on the rafters above their heads were an odd assortment of old computer hardware and UNIX memorabilia. There was an original Macintosh, and various hand held devices that she could not identify. A faded old stuffed Linux penguin named Tux and a baby's bib with the BSD Daemon on it. Joshua's family were definitely geeks. The room was furnished with two plush couches and various wooden end tables. It was comfy and she felt right at home in the cabin. There was a plasma HDTV against the wall where the staircase started. The TV was sitting on a cabinet that held dozens of DVD movies in their original cases. A DVD player was also on the cabinet.

She noticed the remote on the end table and picked it up to turn on the TV.

"Sorry, no channels on that thing, I only use it for watching movies, but I do have a nice stereo back here," he pointed to the desk behind him.

Dancia nodded. "I see." It was a compact little CDROM and AM/FM radio stack with speakers wired all around the room. There was a wooden desk that sat against the wall under the staircase. It had a flat panel monitor and a slim keyboard. "No internet access here either?"

Joshua saw where she was looking. "No actually, that old PC belonged to my dad. I think he had BSD on it; it's an old Pentium. There's a Wi-Fi node at one of the bars downtown. I kind of use this place to get a way from the world as much as possible."

"I didn't know you liked to unplug like this?"

"It helps keep me grounded in reality. It's so easy to become all wrapped up in the everyday details of life. Sometimes, it's good to get away from it all and recharge your batteries."

That was the kind of thing that only people of higher income levels tended to say. Dancia sometimes forgot about how wealthy Joshua actually was. She never asked him about his money, she didn't give it much thought. He didn't flaunt it and so it never really was much of a deal.

"You never mentioned that you had this little cabin before?" she said, motioning to the room they were in with her hand.

"I like to have some secrets."

She looked at him oddly, and then turned on the TV. "Let's watch a movie," she said. She scanned the selection, mostly John Wayne Westerns and just about every Sci-Fi movie made in the last few decades.

"My dad was a John Wayne fan and my mom loved all kinds of Sci-Fi. I like just about anything, I guess."

She pulled out a DVD case and looked at it fondly. "*War Games*, I haven't seen this in ages."

"It's a classic, put it in."

They brought a big wooden bowl full of buttered popcorn and their sodas to the couch and started the movie. They ate and drank and watched the first hour together, making fun of the ancient technology displayed in the film. When the two main characters figured out the password for getting into the war games computer, Dancia looked at Joshua with a serious eye.

"Were you named after that computer?"

Joshua smiled sheepishly. "My parents were geeks. They had just seen the film and both agreed it was a cool name. Not what I would have chosen mind you, but since when does a kid get to choose his own name?"

She laughed. "Don't feel bad, my mother named me after that chick from *The Wonder Years*."

He looked astonished. "Really? Wasn't her name Danica?"

"Yeah well, my dad was dyslexic and he wrote Dancia on the birth certificate. My mother almost killed him but they decided to leave it. At least it spared me comparisons to the race car driver."

They both laughed and snuggled closer together. Joshua unwrapped a blue and orange knit blanket and covered their legs with it. By the time the movie was over, they had missed much of the ending. They were wrapped up in each other's arms, kissing like teenagers.

All those long nights of writing code together, being as close as lovers but never making a move on their desires finally came to a head. He smelling her perfume on his clothes after she had left, her thinking about what it would be like to kiss him as she drove home. Now that she knew what it was like, she wanted more.

Joshua came up for air and noticed the film was over. He stopped the DVD and turned on a lamp on the end table. Dancia sat up and caught her breath. It was better than either had dared dream and they were ready to go further.

Joshua stood up and moved to the back sliding door. The snow was really piling up but he managed to pull it open and stepped outside onto the back deck.

"Where are you going?" Dancia asked. He motioned towards the deck as he used a flat snow shovel to scrape off the top to a hot tub. Dancia smiled, he was crazy. He turned up the water temperature. By the time he came back in the water was hot enough to melt the snowflakes. He came back inside shivering cold and she put the blanket around him.

"It should be warm enough in a few minutes," he said, taking her in his arms and kissing her firmly.

They stood before the glass door, Joshua started by taking off her black rim glasses and setting them on a little table by the door. Her face was thin and delicate, he had never really allowed himself the chance to notice how truly beautiful she was. She pulled off his long sleeved T-shirt and felt the taught muscles of his biceps. She had suspected that he was stronger than he looked and she was right. They finished by stepping out of their underclothes and opening the door. Walking naked out into the driving snowstorm was unbelievably cold. As they sank into the hot tub, the cold was replaced with hot, pulsating water. The contrast was incredible and they laughed as the snow fell around them.

The hot water felt good on their cold bodies. She hovered over him, snow falling in her hair, his warm hands on her waist. She kissed him hard as she lowered herself down on him. They took their time, each savoring the other.

It was awkward as hell trying to make love in a hot tub, but they didn't care. They were too focused on each other to be bothered by the cold, or the hard seats in the tub.

Close to an hour went by before they realized that hunger was creeping up on them again. The sky had gone dark and a few more inches of snow had accumulated around them.

"I guess we should get out of here before we turn into prunes," Joshua said.

"I don't want to get out. I like it right here with you," Dancia whispered into his ear. Her leg was wrapped over his hip and she moved over on top of him. She looked down at him with her dark eyes and her black hair wet on the edges. She was so damn beautiful. He held onto her hips and ran his hands up her back. This time she let him lead and he gently rolled her over. She held onto the padded top of the hot tub as he came out of the water behind her. The cold air mixed with the warm water between them and soon they were oblivious to anything but their desires.

When they had finished the second time, Joshua got up and ran gingerly to the sliding door and pulled it open. Dancia watched him trot naked over to the kitchen and put a pot of water on the stove to cook the noodles. He came back to the glass door and pressed himself against it, making her laugh by leaving three smudges. Then he wrapped himself in a towel and took her the other one. She stepped out of the warm tub and he wrapped her up in the soft towel.

They came inside and dried off. The cabin smelled like an Italian restaurant. Joshua sat down before the circular glass faced fireplace and took out a box of long stem matches. The wood and kindling were already in place and after a few minutes, they had a nice fire going. They took off the towels and snuggled under the blanket on the floor in front of the fire. Lying in each other's arms they were content to watch the embers burn and hold each other tightly.

Hunger finally got the best of them and Joshua got up to put on the noodles. He walked into the closet that was built under the stairs. There was a wine rack near the back of it. He grabbed a flashlight near the door and used it to see the bottles more clearly. There were some nice red wines from the seventies near the back, but he wanted something of a more recent vintage, that would taste good with the meal and not cost him much if they drained it. He found a bottle of French Bordeaux that was only a few years old. Pulling it out of the rack, he used a towel to dust it off. It was one of the first bottles he had purchased after he turned old enough to drink legally. If memory served, this particular wine was not a first growth cult wine but something akin to an average French wine used for everyday meals, perfect for a spaghetti dinner.

Soon the spaghetti noodles were done and they were ready to eat. Joshua ran up stairs again and came down with two bathrobes. They put on the plaid flannel robes and started to get ready for dinner. Joshua fixed a plate of spaghetti and a glass of red wine for each of them and they returned to the fire to eat.

Dancia was not surprised that the spaghetti was delicious she knew Joshua was an excellent cook; it was one of the things she had always liked about him. Cooking was a rare trait in a young man, like finding someone who wrote poetry or could improvise a love song on a guitar. Dancia was at best a modest cook herself. She never really took to traditional female roles, she had been a Tomboy most of her life.

The two of them had completely forgotten why they had come to the cabin in the first place. They were too involved in each other now, to realize that they had not heard from Detective Plait since before noon. Joshua noticed his cell phone on the end table nearest him and suddenly recalled that he had not heard from the police all afternoon. He set his plate down and got up to check the phone. There were no missed calls on it.

"What's wrong?" Dancia asked.

"That detective said he was going to keep me informed on his progress, and I just realized that he hasn't called us all afternoon."

"Maybe the storm is hampering their ability to find Taggert," Dancia offered.

Joshua noticed that the cell phone didn't have a signal at all. No bars. No wonder they didn't get a call.

"That's odd, there's no cell signal. I've always gotten a good signal out here," Joshua said, moving to the island in the kitchen where her cell phone was sitting. Her phone was fully charged and had no signal either.

Dancia went to the wireless phone at the computer desk. She turned it on and got no signal. "The land line's out too," she said, her voice trembling slightly.

Joshua looked around the cabin. *What were the chances of both the cell going down and the landline?* Virtually impossible he guessed. He could imagine that the winter storm might have affected the cell transmission, but not the landline.

Joshua went to the front door of the cabin and opened it a crack, looking out at the snow-covered ground. The Jeep was covered in about one foot of snow and there were no discernible tracks to indicate that a squad car had been by recently. Perhaps the snow had kept the local police from making it out to check on them. It was a relatively small police department and no doubt they were keeping busy with all kinds of winter storm related business.

He locked the front door and padded back down the hall to the main room. Dancia had a worried look on her face as she put her plate down on the table. "Maybe it was the storm? At least we have power."

On cue, the cabin plunged into darkness.

CHAPTER 23

THE UNINTERRUPTIBLE POWER supply for the computer came on with a loud wail. Dancia let out a startled cry. After a second or two the power came back on again. Joshua and Dancia stood there looking at each other for a few moments.

"I guess it was just a flutter," Joshua said, looking around the cabin.

"Scared the hell out of me," Dancia admitted.

She picked up her backpack off the counter and headed for the stairs with it. "I'm going to put some clothes on. Be right back."

Joshua found his clothes on the couch and put them on. He glanced out the windows and got an eerie feeling that someone was watching him. He couldn't see far in the snowstorm so he dismissed it.

As Dancia walked up the stairs to the second floor she looked up at all the family pictures on display. There were pictures of Joshua as a little boy and then a young man. She figured he had a pretty awesome childhood.

The master bedroom was most of the top floor over the living room and the kitchen. It had a solid wall of windows that faced the river and huge dark wooden beams that angled down sharply from the steep A-frame roof.

Dancia flipped on the light switch and set the backpack down on the bed. Unzipping the pack, she pulled out a blouse and some jeans and underwear.

Taking off her robe she stepped into her underpants. As she was about to put on her blouse something bit her in the side. She absently swiped at the sting. She expected to remove some kind of a bug. Her hand came up with blood on it. She had been shot. In that fleeting moment she had just enough awareness and training to throw herself to the floor.

A second shot pierced the glass windows. It impacted the bedpost. Wood shattered. Dancia dragged herself behind the bed for cover.

"Joshua, shots fired!"

No response. The power went out again. The battery backup screamed like a siren. She lay there for a few moments, holding her side to stop the bleeding.

All the time she was in Iraq she had never been shot. Friends of hers had been shot, blown up and captured by insurgents but she had escaped injury. Until now. She had always been afraid that she would be shot and not killed. She didn't think that she had the guts to stay alert and alive after getting grievously wounded. Despite her tough girl persona, she was a real wimp when it came to pain.

Lying on her left side, she was already getting light headed. The bullet passed clean through her. The exit wound was little more than the size of her pinky finger. Her adrenaline was pumping. Her head was surprisingly clear and calm. She knew she had to apply pressure to the wound. She started looking around for something to plug the hole and let her blood clot.

"Shit, it hurts," she mumbled.

There were no more shots coming at her but she feared that Joshua would be next. She lay on her back and shouted down the hall. "Joshua, I'm shot!"

/*--*/

Joshua wanted to respond to Dancia's plea, but the dark figure at
the back door was holding a pistol and looking right at him. The
man opened the glass door and stepped inside. *Damn, I forgot
to lock the stupid door!* Joshua felt stupid for letting his guard
down. Sweat started to bead on his forehead. The man seemed
completely relaxed, as if he had just come in from a walk.

"Smells good, just the way your mother used to make it,"
Taggert said.

/*--*/

Dancia had her ear to the floor and she heard someone talking.
It was not Joshua, so she decided to be quiet.

She found her shirt on the bed and used it to stuff into the
hole in her side. Her hands were bloody and there was a small
pool of red on the green shag carpet. The pain came and went in
relation to how much she moved. She got still again, listening
to the floor.

/*--*/

Joshua could see Taggert's lean face lit from a sudden flare up
in the fireplace. The last log he put on finally caught fire and lit
the room well enough to see what Taggert was wearing. He had
a black watch cap on and a solid green guide parka, black ski
pants and black GORE-TEX boots. There was a hunting rifle
with a scope strapped to his shoulder. Snow was melting fast off
his parka and cap as he faced Joshua in a relaxed stance.

Taggert noticed Joshua's nervous glance upwards. "Don't
worry, I only grazed her. She'll be alright," he said without
concern.

"How many people are you going to kill Larry?" Joshua
asked.

"Oh, just about one more, I reckon."

Taggert walked over towards Joshua, who slowly backed off
towards the kitchen. There was a chef's knife still on the island

cutting board. Joshua tried not to look at it. Taggert picked up a fork and motioned to the spaghetti. Joshua nodded consent. Taggert took a large bite of the still warm spaghetti and chewed it slowly.

"Good, very tasty. A tad too much oregano for my taste, but not bad."

"Finish it, if you want," Joshua said.

Taggert put the fork down and turned to Joshua. "I didn't come here to eat. I came hear to kill you."

Joshua moved slowly behind the counter, keeping something solid between him and Taggert. He tried to remain calm, which was damn near impossible after what Taggert had just said.

"But first things first. Just how exactly did you figure out it was me who killed Zemo and Glenn?" Taggert patiently waited for an answer. He gave no inclination that he was ready to shoot Joshua. Joshua stammered through his explanation, using his hands to nervously punctuate what he said.

"Ah, well. We originally had thought you were Shemp. But, I heard you two talking on the radio about making another hit and then you attacked Dancia."

Taggert held up a hand to stop him. "Wait, how did you know I was using the radio to communicate with Shemp?"

"One of you let the frequency slip in the chat room."

Taggert looked thoughtful. "It was just a number, how did you deduce that it was a frequency?"

"I have a friend who is a Ham and he told me it could be a forty meter frequency. After that we just listened every night until we heard you talking." Joshua didn't want to divulge too much about what they had done. He didn't want to put his friends in jeopardy too.

"I see. How did you discover the methodology I used? I assume you examined Glenn's computer closely."

Joshua was starting to get concerned for Dancia. She had not made any noise since she had called down to him and he wondered if she was still alive up stairs.

"Yes. I found your calling card in the code. Why did you do that?"

Taggert moved slowly back towards the couch and the fireplace. Joshua watched him and didn't move, waiting for the right moment to grab the knife on the chopping block.

"I had to convince you that Glenn was murdered and that you might be next, so that you would begin your search for his killer. You see it was you that I wanted all along. Killing Glenn and that other kid was just to get you involved. I must say, you did a bang up job. Tell me something though, how did you discover that I was using an iTunes exploit to get your girlfriend?"

Joshua shrugged. "Oldest trick in the book, buffer overflow to a null pointer. Take down the application and replace it with a compromised version. What had me confused was how you got them hypnotized. I thought you were using Flash animation. But that was not your style. You're a Perl guy, Larry. Like so many other masters of a single language, you tend to use it to solve every problem." He was taking a risk in angering Taggert with that remark.

Taggert shrugged. "I actually used a good bit of C on this exploit. Perl is divine but even it has limitations."

Joshua nodded. He looked down at the knife and wanted so badly to sneak it off the table somehow. He forced himself to remain calm and patient.

"I suppose you are wondering why I have gone to such extremes just to kill you?" Taggert turned to look at Joshua again, the light from the fire giving a warm glow to his harsh face.

"The thought had crossed my mind."

Taggert walked slowly over to the island, he still held the pistol relaxed in his hand. "Did your parents ever tell you anything about me while you were growing up?"

"No. I think I always knew that you guys used to know each

other, but that's about it."

Taggert smiled. "Interesting. Let me tell you a story about a boy, a girl and another boy."

Joshua was listening, but he was not sure whether to believe what he was hearing. "Your father and I went to school together in Florida. We both got into computers and programming before Gates and Jobs were out of diapers. We saw where things were headed even if nobody else seemed to realize it. Your father had a good eye for coding. Did you know he created his own language while in school?"

Joshua shook his head.

"It was crude and not very flexible but I built him a compiler for it and we soon became rather close friends. He was dating your mother back then, the two were inseparable. He had to go off for an internship one semester and while the cat was away, your mom and I played."

Joshua could not believe he was hearing this crap about his parents. But he pretended to be interested to buy himself time to think of something. Taggert went on about how he and Joshua's mother had screwed around and when his father got back in town the truth got out.

"Your father was not a very forgiving man. He told me one night that if I ever tried to make a move on his girl again, he would flat out kill me."

"You're crazy! My father would never threaten anyone like that. He was the kindest person I've ever known," Joshua said defiantly.

Taggert was taking particular pleasure in revealing the story to Joshua. He started strolling around the cabin, looking at things as he told his tale. "If any of us knew our parents as they were before we were born, I'm sure it would give us all a chill. He was in love and he was young. I knew when I was not wanted and I stopped seeing both of them. Besides, I knew your mother didn't really like me like she loved your father. We eventually graduated and got jobs out in the real world. I thought I had seen the last of both of them, until they got engaged.

"Your father invited me to their wedding in Idaho. He had his bachelor party right here in this very cabin. We fished the river. Back then there actually were fish in it and we even went hunting." He stopped next to a wall of pictures. Looked closely at one and then took it off the wall and tossed it like a Frisbee to Joshua.

"Here we are on the back porch with the buck that your father shot."

Joshua looked closely at the picture. Five men were standing in front of a fallen buck. Joshua had seen the picture on that wall all his life but he never knew who some of the men were until now. One was Taggert. He was even holding the same hunting riffle that he now had on him.

Taggert pulled off his watch cap and set it down on the computer desk. He touched the computer keyboard with his fingers, ever so gently. "This is an old UNIX keyboard. Your dad always preferred the positive feedback and the no arrow keys layout." Taggert seemed lost in thought looking at the gray and white keys.

Joshua eyed the knife again, moving closer to it, trying to think of a way to use it to defend him. If he were a hero in a movie, he would just pick it up and throw it into Taggert and kill him. But he was not an action hero; he was just a geek. It was not in his nature or his realm of experience to attack and kill anyone.

Taggert turned back to face Joshua. "Your father used to be a very smart and gifted programmer. But after the wedding, he seemed to become more involved in management and spent less time actually coding. He rose quickly in the ranks at RegTech, moving from one division to another, gaining more responsibilities, earning more and growing in popularity within the company.

"Eventually, he never came around slumming with us grunts in the trenches anymore. It wasn't expected of him by upper management I'm sure. But before long the company started to make business decisions that were more based on profit than technological know-how. They started to take away benefits and even retirement plans. RegTech grew into the faceless, international company that it is now."

Taggert began to walk around the room again, his back to Joshua for a brief time. In that moment, Joshua grabbed the knife with his right hand and held it behind the island. Joshua's palms were wet with sweat as he held the handle of the chef's knife firmly. It was his father's favorite kitchen knife. It had a heavy blade and a thick handle for big hands to easily grip.

Taggert moved in front of the fireplace and turned to face Joshua. He shifted the pistol in his hands as if it were getting heavy.

"This is all very interesting Larry, but it doesn't explain why you want to kill me."

Taggert grinned wryly. "My pension was just dropped. They are making me retire early by offering me a buy-out. It's cheaper for them to send me packing with some cash than to provide for me in retirement. I got nothing left. No job, no retirement and no respect from punk coders like yourself.

"Your father was a brilliant programmer. But I was better than him, more intelligent, more insightful and more creative. Your father's analytical skills were impressive but he let them wither on the vine when he went into management. We used to play chess with each other, even after he left our engineering team. We used to tie each other more often then not. After he got married and we drifted apart, his game became less precise, more distracted. He no longer coded at all and before long, I was beating him nearly every time we played chess."

Joshua was becoming distracted from what Taggert was saying by thoughts of what had happened to Dancia. *Was she still alive? Was she waiting for some opportune time to come down stairs? Could she even walk?* He told himself to calm down and stay focused on what Taggert was saying. He squeezed the knife in his hand and tried to think of a way to disarm Taggert. Joshua was a pacifist by nature. He was not interested in killing Taggert, only disarming him and letting the police do the dangerous stuff. But the police were not here and he was bringing a knife to a gunfight. Not the smartest thing he had ever done.

"What are you getting at Larry?"

Taggert's eyes narrowed as he stopped talking for a moment. "You are smarter than your father ever was. I've seen your code; it's not brilliant. But you have very keen powers of observation and an intuition for things that make you a formidable opponent. Not everyone would have figured out that Shemp and I were communicating via Ham Radio or that he was my Stooge, as you said.

"I have very much enjoyed our little cat and mouse game and I suspect that deep down inside, you have enjoyed it too." Taggert's lips curled into a twisted grin that made him look truly disturbed.

Joshua had to admit to himself that the past few days had been exciting in an intellectual kind of way. But he was not getting off on it in the same way that Taggert apparently was. For Joshua, he was avenging the death of a coworker and trying to protect his own butt. For Taggert it was some kind of a game that stimulated his ego more than anything.

"You're a sick man Larry. But I'm not as smart as you thought. I let you trap me here in the middle of a storm with no way to defend myself. Sorry I was not a better opponent for you."

"You were good enough, son. Good enough to keep me amused for some time. That's about all I can expect out of anyone."

Joshua couldn't believe how egotistical that sounded, like he was so superior to everyone else on the planet. It made him want to defeat Taggert just to bring him down a notch. But it did not make him want to kill the man. Despite what he had done to Zemo and Glenn. Despite what he had done to Dancia.

Taggert knew this. He knew that he could not get Joshua to hate him by killing his coworker or wounding his girlfriend or even by insulting his father and slandering his mother. He knew that there was only one thing that would push Joshua Jones over the edge and make him go on the offensive. He was saving it for his final play, his check move that would force his opponent into action.

"Your parents did not die by accident on that mountain road. The brakes on their car were rigged to fail when they needed them," Taggert said.

"*I* killed your parents, Joshua Jones."

Joshua's anger clouded his face.

"John turned away from the code and became just another cog in the wheel of a big, heartless machine that is RegTech. I saved him from himself."

"You are one twisted son-of-a-bitch, Taggert."

CHAPTER 24

DANCIA GATHERED HER strength and carefully stood up, using the bed to steady herself. Her head swam around for a moment as she fought to remain conscious.

She kept pressure to her wound with her right hand as she unzipped the backpack and pulled out a belt and a T-shirt. She folded up the T-shirt and applied it directly to her wound. Then she loosened a thin black belt and strapped it around her waist. Pulling the belt tight sent another sharp pain through her body. She pulled out a second shirt and carefully put it on.

She could hear Taggert talking down stairs but she was unable to pick out what he was saying. *He was damn windy.* Reaching into the pack she pulled out the Colt pistol. *I'll have to see about shutting him up, permanently.*

Dancia took a pillow and put it over the gun on the bed. Then she pulled the slide back and chambered a round. The Colt was not an easy weapon to handle. It was heavy, intended to be used in combat by strong male soldiers.

She edged her way out of the room using the doorway to help keep her upright. Her fingers gripped the heavy pistol. At the top of the stairs she could hear what Taggert was saying. He had just confessed to killing Joshua's parents. Dancia swallowed hard. She took the first step down the carpeted stairs. *Oh God, please don't let me fall. All I have to do is get down far enough for a good shot at him.* The fire made crackling sounds that helped mask her footsteps.

She decided to lie down on the stairs, partly to lower her profile and partly because she was finding it hard to keep from passing out. As she took the second step, a sharp pain radiated from her side. She lost her footing and fell.

Taggert heard the commotion and spun around. He brought his pistol up as Dancia's body tumbled down the stairs and came to rest in a pile against a bookshelf. She didn't move after falling. Her pistol was safely tucked under her back. Taggert took a quick look back at Joshua and saw the concern on his face but he was not moving.

Taggert edged towards the base of the stairs to see if the girl was conscious. He poked her with his boot, his back to Joshua. Joshua brought up the chef's knife and threw it over handed as hard as he could at Taggert. Taggert saw movement in his peripheral vision and stepped back out of the way as the heavy knife sailed past him. It bounced pathetically off the paneled wall of the cabin.

What the hell else can I throw at this bastard? The counter was empty. He wanted to kill Tagger and didn't much care how. Seeing nothing useful, he ducked down behind the island.

"Nice try kid. I didn't think you would go for the knife."

Joshua's heart was pounding in his chest. He tried to hear Taggert's foot steps to see which side of the island he would come around. But Taggert was not moving. He picked up the chef's knife and examined it closely.

"This was your father's favorite cooking knife was it not? I don't think he would have approved of you tossing it around like that. Not good for the edge."

Joshua swore to himself under his breath. "He would have approved of me OJ'ing your ass with it."

Taggert laughed out loud. "Perhaps."

Joshua opened the cabinet door to the island and looked

inside for something to use to kill Taggert with. There was an old iron skillet that looked heavy enough to crush a skull, if he got close enough. But that probably would not happen. He took it out carefully anyway, thinking it may work well enough to catch a slug.

"You never asked me if I had tried to attack you on your computer, Joshua," Taggert taunted.

Joshua tried to think back over the past few days to see if he had in fact been attacked and did not realize it. He found it incredibly difficult to think straight through his bitter hatred.

"When did you first start having nightmares about your parent's death? A week after they died, I attacked you over your computer. I put feelings of guilt into your head about distracting your father. You didn't cause him to loose control on that icy road, he would have lost control at some point and his brakes would not have saved him. But I made you think it was your fault. For the past six years, I tweaked my system and played hell with your psyche in the process. How does that make you feel?"

"What do you think, you bastard?"

Joshua tightened his grip on the old iron skillet's handle. *How could anyone be so maniacal? All this time I believed I was responsible for my parent's death. All those damn sleepless nights and horrible dreams. It was all an implanted memory. Fuck him, he's so dead.*

"You might as well just stand up and take it like a man," Taggert said. He moved slowly towards the kitchen, handgun at the ready.

Joshua could hear Taggert's footsteps and knew that he was coming around the far side of the island. Joshua edged himself around the island to keep himself hidden. There really wasn't much of a chance, but he was trying to buy himself some time. *Maybe the police will finally show? Fat chance that will happen,* Joshua thought. *If they haven't come by now they never will. They probably think Taggert is still in Boise.*

"Come on kid, stand up and let's get this over with. I can't linger here much longer, got the State Police, FBI and half the county looking for me."

"They will find you, Larry, and then what will you do?" Joshua asked.

Taggert stopped at the other side of the island. He took aim and fired a shot into the floor just shy of Joshua's feet. Joshua pulled up his feet reflexively.

"They won't find me. I'm too smart for that," Taggert said.

Dancia regained consciousness and lifted her head up. She could see Taggert moving closer to Joshua, who was hiding behind the kitchen island. She felt the cold pistol underneath her and reached for it with her right hand. The pain in her side was intense and her head was throbbing. The T-shirt covering her wound was sopped with her blood. She appeared to have avoided injury when she fell, other than knocking her head against the bookshelf. She slipped the lever of the safety off and raised the pistol toward Taggert. She had a shot, but it was not good enough for a kill shot.

Taggert pointed the pistol toward the opposite end of the island and shot at Joshua's head. Joshua was already cowering on the opposite side, anticipating the shot. Joshua turned around and saw her sitting up slowly and pointing the heavy pistol at Taggert. He was relieved that she was alive and holding the gun.

She rolled the pistol around in a nod to get him to move around to the other side of the island. He looked confused at first and then seemed to figure out what she was getting at.

Taggert made it easy on her, he moved forward slowly. His back was to Dancia and she sat up straighter to get a clear shot. The Marine in her wanted to get behind some cover but she had to settle for bracing her arm against the wooden banister.

"Got any last requests, kid?" Taggert asked as he brought the pistol up for a killing shot and took a step forward.

"Yeah, as a matter fact I do."

Joshua slowly stood up with his hands raised above his head

and stared into the eyes of his killer. Taggert aimed square at Joshua's chest.

"When you see my parents, give them my love, asshole."

Taggert looked confused. Joshua gave him a raw grin with his teeth clenched. Taggert's puzzled face tightened and then his eyes grew wide.

Dancia aimed the pistol and fired. The shot rang out in the tiny cabin like a canon firing. Joshua stood his ground as the shot grazed Taggert's side, spinning him around as the forty-five-caliber bullet ripped through him. Taggert brought the Beretta up and pointed it at Dancia. Before he could get a shot off, Joshua leaped over the island with the iron skillet and brought it down hard against Taggert's head. Taggert fell to the ground facing Dancia.

Taggert's skull was cracked on the initial impact but he continued in vain to try and aim the pistol at Dancia. Joshua sat astride Taggert's back and brought the iron skillet down again and again as all of his pent up rage exploded in a violent bashing. When he finally stopped, there was nothing left of the back of Taggert's head. He dropped the skillet and pushed off the dead man's back.

Dancia dropped the Colt pistol and fell back against the bookcase. She almost passed out again from the pain, but the smell of cordite kept her conscious. The gun had jolted her pretty well when it fired. Joshua stood up, his knees wobbly. It was over. Taggert was dead.

Joshua ran over to Dancia and put his hand behind her head. She looked up at him and smiled. They kissed passionately, both thankful to be alive and together. When they parted she motioned to Taggert.

"You're pretty good with a skillet, for a guy."

"We've got to get you some help. Can you move?"

She shook her head. "I best not. The pain is killing me."

Joshua looked back at the kitchen. He thought about the cell phone signal and the power being out. He walked over to

Taggert and looked out the kitchen window. The streetlight at
the circle down the road was on, meaning that the neighborhood
actually had power. He could probably walk up the street and
find someone home. His foot touched the butt of Taggert's
pistol. He bent down and pulled the pistol out from under the
man's torso, trying not to look at the gory mess of bone and flesh
that used to be Taggert's head.

Joshua put the Beretta on the kitchen island and then he
noticed something sticking out of Taggert's parka. A narrow
black antenna. Joshua pulled out the hand held device. A
portable cell phone jammer. He turned it off and then picked up
his cell phone on the counter top. It had a full signal and he had
half a dozen calls waiting on him.

He dialed the last number, one that he knew to be detective
Plait. The phone rang only once before Plait answered it.

"This is Plait."

"You can send in the cavalry now. We have Taggert here and
he's dead," Joshua said.

"Kid, are you all right? I've got half the state heading for
your cabin!"

Joshua stepped back toward Dancia. "I hope that includes
an ambulance. Dancia's been shot, she needs medical help."

Plait barked orders into his radio at two different agencies.
"Ok, we're about a mile out of McCall. Stay put, help is on the
way."

"Perfect," Joshua said.

"You say you have Taggert there?" Plait asked.

"Yes, but he's dead. Just get here as fast as you can." Joshua
closed his phone and slammed it down hard. He was still pissed
at Taggert for having shot Dancia.

"How did you get the phone to work?" Dancia asked.

"He was using a cell phone jamming device. The police are
on the way. How are you doing?"

She managed a weak grin. "I'll live."

Joshua was thankful for that, more than she would ever

know. He sat down behind her and held her gently in his arms. They could hear sirens in the distance, as Joshua rested his chin on Dancia's shoulder.

The silver Porsche edged off the road near a pull out and came to a stop. There was still crusted snow on the ground but it had not snowed since the late November blizzard. The Payette River was running despite being frozen in some spots. Joshua got out of the car and went around opening the door for Dancia. She got out slowly, still recovering from her wound. He helped her walk with him over to the river's edge.

She was wearing a dark winter coat and gloves, her black hair pulled back under a scarf. He was wearing his heavy overcoat and driving gloves. He pulled out a small porcelain jar and squatted at the river's edge. It contained the cremated remains of Unix his family's cat. He had lived a long and happy life and Joshua felt the need to release him at the same spot he had let go of his parents six years before.

He opened the jar and poured the gray ashes into the cold water of the river. As he watched the powder swirl around in the current he said a silent goodbye to the cat and to his mother and father. He no longer clung to his guilt. He was finally at peace with their passing. There was an inner calm that came with knowing that they were not killed in an accident caused by him. There was an even greater calm in knowing that their killer was now dead.

Joshua was free.

CHAPTER 25

JOSHUA DROPPED THE mail on his counter and sorted through it. Underneath the usual assortment of bills and junk mail, was a large manila envelope. It was from Detective Bill Plait of the Boise Police Department.

Joshua had asked Plait to send him the police report from his parent's accident. Joshua stared at the envelope for a moment before opening it. He had to know for sure whether the brake lines had been tampered with on his parent's car.

He opened the envelope and slid out the photocopied police report. Plait had marked out some department internal details but the report was largely untouched. He sat down in the chair at the kitchen table where the old radio still sat. He skimmed over the gruesome details from the coroner and found the parts where the car was pulled from the river and inspected by Police Department mechanics.

Except for the damage to the front end of the car from impact with the water, the car was found to be in perfect mechanical order. The brake lines were even looked at closely by the lead mechanic and two wheels were found to have loose brake calipers; the mechanical clamps that closed on the disc brakes and created friction. In the opinion of the senior mechanic, that was not enough to have caused the accident. The brakes were in working order and had not failed.

The accident really was an accident. Taggert had thought

he had disabled the brakes but apparently his efforts to cause the accident had failed.

Joshua sat back and put his hands on his head, staring at the ceiling before closing his eyes. He was beginning to feel a headache coming on. *What really happened on that day five years ago? Did he actually distract his father or had Taggert implanted that memory?* Nothing was clear to him anymore. Try as he might, he could not remember the accident clearly enough to remove all of his guilt.

Suddenly his life was complicated again, just when he thought he had found peace.

Acknowledgements

Thanks to all my writer friends at Partner's in Crime, whose support and mentoring have been and continue to be invaluable to me. Several co-workers of mine have read this book and contributed their comments and opinions. Many thanks to Joyce Popp, Jeremy Carey Dressler, Jeremy Reeder, Mike Hachigian and Jeff Love for reading the early drafts and telling me where I was screwing up both with the story and with the technical details. A special thank you to Bill Blohm and his wife Debbie, for their contributions and support. I am especially grateful to Angela Abderhalden for her careful copy edits and wise suggestions.

For another outstanding cover design and interior layout, I once again thank my brother Byron. You always make my words look great, even if they are not always great words. As always, I would like to thank my wonderful wife Laurie, for her support and understanding of my writing habit.

www.ingramcontent.com/pod-product-compliance
Lightning Source LLC
Chambersburg PA
CBHW020949180626
46814CB00003B/1006